NANCY DREW

girl detective ™

#19

The Orchid Thief

CAROLYN KEENE

Aladdin Paperbacks

New York   London   Toronto   Sydney

❧ALADDIN PAPERBACKS
An imprint of Simon & Schuster Children's Publishing Division
1230 Avenue of the Americas, New York, NY 10020
Copyright © 2006 by Simon & Schuster, Inc.
All rights reserved, including the right of
reproduction in whole or in part in any form.
NANCY DREW is a registered trademark of Simon & Schuster, Inc.
ALADDIN PAPERBACKS, NANCY DREW: GIRL DETECTIVE, and
colophon are trademarks of Simon & Schuster, Inc.
Manufactured in the United States of America
First Aladdin Paperbacks edition September 2006
10 9 8 7 6 5 4 3 2 1
Library of Congress Control Number 2005934878
ISBN-13: 978-1-4169-0980-4
ISBN-10: 1-4169-0980-X

Fishy Doings

"Is something wrong?" Bess asked, glancing at the boat.

"I'm not sure," Delia said, her eyes still fixed on the other boat. "It's just odd that he stopped when he saw us."

The driver of the red boat was too far away to see clearly. The brim of his baseball cap hid most of his face. All I saw was a blue T-shirt and dark cap. Then, all at once, I heard the buzz-saw sound of the engine revving. The boat spun around in a U-turn and flew back down the tiny channel.

Talk about alarm bells. About a zillion of them went off inside my head. "What's he running from?" I wondered.

"Us. At least I think so. He must have spotted my uniform," Delia said. "And trust me, the only people who run from parks employees are the ones who are up to no good."

NANCY DREW
girl detective™

Available from Aladdin Paperbacks

Contents

Island Intrigue

You're totally hopeless, Nancy. We've been in Florida for less than an hour, and you've already gotten us lost!"

My friend Bess Marvin was the one doing the talking. And she was right about me being hopeless. When my mind is on a mystery, I'm useless behind the wheel. I get so busy trying to figure things out that I forget about practical details like keeping track of directions. So I guess it's no surprise that I always end up getting lost on some back road I've never seen before.

Like right now, for instance.

Now that Bess had shaken me from my thoughts, I realized I must have turned off Route 1. That's the main road our friend Delia Duke had told us to take

1

from Miami down to Key Largo, the first in a chain of tropical islands that curve out from the southern tip of Florida. After spending the morning on a plane from Chicago—the closest big city to our hometown of River Heights—I couldn't wait to get there.

But now it looked like the drive might take a little longer than we'd expected—okay, maybe a lot longer. I didn't see any of the things I'd noticed along Route 1 before—malls or fast-food joints or housing developments, or even any traffic lights. There was just a narrow, cracked road that stretched in an endless straight line ahead of us. Next to the road, the ground sloped down to mangrove swamps on both sides that spread out as far as the eye could see. The baking-hot sun sent heat waves shimmering up from the asphalt and glared off the murky water surrounding the mangrove roots. Except for a couple of trucks in the hazy distance—and maybe some alligators—we were totally alone.

"Uh-oh," I said, biting my lip. "Guess I made a wrong turn, huh?"

"You think?" Bess's cousin George Fayne said sarcastically from the backseat of our rental car. As she leaned forward, a hot, humid wind whipped over the windshield and sent her short hair flying around her face. "Not to mention that it's about a zillion degrees out. I never should have let you talk us into renting

2

this convertible, Bess. Shouldn't we at least put up the top and turn on the air conditioning?"

"And give up a second of soaking up this glorious tropical sun?" Bess slid her sunglasses to the top of her head and shot her cousin a horrified glance. "Not a chance! This salty air feels great, and if we can smell the ocean, we can't be *too* lost, can we?"

"Oh, brother," said George, flopping back against her seat.

I had to laugh. Even though Bess and George are cousins, they're polar opposites in the looks and personality departments. Bess is petite with long blond hair. A total dreamer, she can find the silver lining in any cloud. George is way more down-to-earth. She loves sports and keeps her dark hair short. But somehow she and Bess always manage to work out their differences— which is good for me, since I've been best friends with both of them practically since the three of us learned to walk.

"This is a record, even for you, Nancy," George went on, staring out at the tangled mangrove swamp. "You don't usually get car-challenged until *after* you start working a mystery."

Ouch. I guess she had a point. Delia hadn't said for sure that we'd find any mystery in Key Largo. But she'd definitely hinted at it.

"You have to admit, hearing from Delia out of the

blue was kind of strange," I said. "Even though she grew up down the street from Dad and me, we've hardly seen her since she left River Heights to go to college here in Florida. That was, what, four or five years ago? And when she called, she did say she might need our help with something."

"So naturally you decided to start obsessing about it before we even find out what the problem is," Bess teased. "Don't forget, she also said there might not be anything to worry about at all. Which means we're in for a week of fun in the sun while we catch up on all Delia's been doing the past couple of years."

"If we ever find our way to Key Largo, that is," George added.

Bess and George like to tease me, but I don't think they *really* mind when I've got a mystery on the brain. They're used to this sort of thing. Plus, they're a huge help. If there's one thing they do agree on, it's that I'd be lost without them.

"Maybe I can figure out where we are," George said. She was already reaching for the laptop case that lay on the seat next to her. "There's this great mapping system I can log on to."

"Hear that, Nancy?" Bess said, flicking a thumb at her cousin. "Most girls bring sunscreen and a bikini to the beach. George brings a computer."

George grinned and said, "A vacation isn't a

vacation without my laptop. You know that."

Bess just rolled her eyes and reached into her bag for her cell phone. "I'd better call Delia and tell her we're . . . wherever we are," she said.

Hearing that, I felt an uneasiness bubble up inside of me. Delia had sounded kind of stressed when I called her from the airport. I didn't want to add to her worries. "Couldn't we just—"

"Yes!" George crowed from the backseat. "You can put away that phone, Bess. I just pinpointed where we are. According to my mapping system, this is Card Sound Road. The Card Sound Bridge should be coming up soon. It's an alternate route to Key Largo." She flashed me a smile in the rearview mirror. "It'll take us a little longer to get to the state park where Delia works, but we're not too far off track. I've got the directions right here."

Sure enough, a few minutes later we caught sight of a high-arching bridge ahead. We cruised past a tiny village of house boats at the edge of the swamp, and then we rose up and over a sparkling deep-blue bay.

"How gorgeous!" Bess exclaimed.

George and I weren't going to argue with her. I felt like I was looking at a postcard, complete with sailboats, swaying palms, and herons perched on mangrove branches. As pretty as it was, the sight I was happiest to see was a plain green sign at the end of the bridge that read WELCOME TO KEY LARGO.

"We made it! Thanks, George," I said.

"Am I good, or what? Turn right at the light, Nan," she told me. "We'll be back on Route 1 in a flash."

Pretty soon, the dense trees gave way to a sun-bleached strip of motels, restaurants, tourist boutiques, bait-and-tackle shops, boat rentals, and places advertising scuba, snorkeling, and fishing expeditions. Bess raised an eyebrow as we passed a Jeep full of tanned guys with Hawaiian shirts and windblown hair.

"This is more like it," she said. "No wonder Delia decided to stay here in Florida after college!"

"I don't think she came *just* for the guys," George commented dryly. "There are tons of exotic plants and animals around here. Not to mention amazing tropical fish that live around the coral reef. People come from all over to see it. It's the perfect place for a marine biologist like Delia."

From what I had read, the coral reef *was* amazing. It stretched alongside the Florida Keys from Key Largo all the way down to Key West at the very end of Route 1—a hundred miles away. Delia had told us a big chunk of the reef lay inside the state park where she worked, and she'd promised to show us the best snorkeling and scuba-diving spots. It sounded like the perfect way to spend our week with Delia. Still, I couldn't help wondering what Delia meant when she'd said something weird was going on.

"Earth to Nancy! Didn't you see the sign for the state park? Delia told us to meet her there, right?"

Ooops! I couldn't believe I had spaced out again. I pulled myself back to reality in time to see a sign for the John Pennekamp Coral Reef State Park out of the corner of my eye. "Right! Sorry, Bess," I said, shifting into the turn lane. Seconds later we cruised into the entrance.

I pulled to the end of a long line of sedans, minivans, and SUVs. None of them were moving. A blaring horn made me jump, and I heard someone shout, "Hey! Quit blocking the way!"

"What's the problem?" Bess wondered. But a black SUV in front of us meant we had zero visibility.

I got out of our car and stepped around the SUV. We were about ten cars back from the entrance gate. A truck had stopped there and the driver had gotten out. He was waving his arms at the entrance worker, and neither one of them looked very happy.

"Why doesn't he move to the side? There's enough room," I muttered. I was already heading toward the entrance gate. "Excuse me!" I called. "Ma'am? Sir?"

Neither the entrance worker nor the man who had gotten out of his truck heard me. They were too busy arguing to notice anyone else.

"I told you, sir. I can't let you in unless you pay the fee," the woman inside the booth was saying. She gave an annoyed tug at the green collar of her parks uniform. "Now, if you don't move your truck, I'll have to call security. . . ."

The driver of the truck stood with his back to me, so all I saw were long baggy shorts, a broad back covered with an orange T-shirt, and sun-bleached blond hair that peeked out from under his black baseball cap. "You can't keep me out of here," he drawled. "My folks have been on the Keys since before Florida was even a state!"

"You still have to pay, like everyone else," the entrance worker said patiently.

"Excuse me!" I said again, louder.

This time, both the entrance worker and the driver of the truck turned toward me. Except the guy did more than just look. His eyes were like green lasers that zeroed in on every detail.

"Well, hello there! What can I do for you, ma'am?" he asked. A slow smile spread across his face.

Oh, brother. I could tell he was used to turning on the charm. I just wanted to get past him so we could find Delia. "I, um, my friends and I need to get in to see Delia Duke," I began. "She's expecting us. Would you mind moving your truck?"

The guy glanced over his shoulder at the beat-up blue pickup truck that blocked the park entrance. Actually, it wasn't *totally* blue. Silver paint covered a couple of dings along the side, and the rear left fender was dented and painted silver.

"Why should I?" he said. "I have every right to be here. And I don't appreciate a couple of tourists trying to muscle into the park ahead of me."

He was still smiling, but his eyes had a challenging gleam in them now. He didn't make a move to leave. "You give Delia Duke a message from me, okay?" he went on. "You tell her that Chick Russell does what he wants, where he wants, when he wants. And a nosy out-of-towner like her isn't going to stop me."

At that moment something jump-started in my brain. I guess you could call it a sixth sense, a kind of signal that I needed to pay close attention.

"Do you know Delia?" I asked him.

"Just tell her what I said," he replied.

"That's it. I'm calling security," muttered the entrance worker.

Chick Russell's gaze flickered from the woman inside the booth to me. He must not have wanted to go head-to-head with parks police, because he sauntered back to his truck and climbed in behind the wheel.

"You take care now," he said, tipping his baseball cap at me.

He pulled his truck in a U-turn around the booth to the exit on the other side. Then he turned onto Route 1 and was gone.

Message from a Conch

I was still staring after the beat-up blue truck when Bess and George pulled up at the entrance booth in our convertible.

"Hop in!" George called from behind the wheel.

"Um, are you all right, Nancy?" Bess added.

"Yeah . . . fine." I shook myself and climbed into the backseat. "There was something weird about the guy in that truck, that's all."

"The one that was blocking the entrance? What happened?" asked Bess.

Now that Chick Russell was gone, I wasn't sure what to make of what he had said. "He gave me a message for Delia. Maybe it was nothing. I'll tell you about it when we get to her office."

The main drive led past dense trees to a big parking lot near the water. Beyond the lot was a small beach with a store and concession stand, and a strip of land that led to a marina where some tour boats were docked. There was a salty tang in the air, and the perfumed smell of some kind of tropical flower. Mangrove trees grew so thickly around the marina that a channel had been cleared so boats could get to the open water beyond the trees.

"It's paradise!" Bess exclaimed, after we found a spot and got out of the car. She breathed in deeply, gazing at the palm trees, mangroves, and sparkling blue water.

I could tell George liked what she saw too. She's not the bubbly, gushing type, but there was a definite spark of interest in her eye when she spotted a couple carrying scuba equipment toward the marina.

"Delia works at the Visitor Center, right?" I said. Shading my eyes from the sun, I scanned the low wooden buildings that dotted the ground between the beach and the marina. "It's got to be around here somewhere. . . ."

"Nancy! Bess! George! Over here!"

We whirled around to see Delia waving to us from the doorway of a boxlike building near the marina. It had been about two years since we'd seen her, but she hadn't changed. She still had the same wide smile, the same black hair just long enough to tuck behind her ears, and the same warm energy that seemed to radiate from her as she ran over to give us hugs.

"I'm glad you made it. I was starting to worry that maybe you got lost," she told us.

"We did, thanks to Nancy 'Space Cadet' Drew here," George said, nodding at me.

"And then we were further delayed by some guy at the entrance," Bess added.

"Actually, I think you might know him, Delia. He said to give you a message," I said.

As we walked back toward the Visitor Center, I told her what Chick Russell had said. The second she heard his name Delia's smile faded. "I know Chick, all right. We've had a couple of run-ins here at the park," she said. "We've got strict laws protecting the wildlife at Pennekamp, but I'm afraid Chick doesn't care much for rules and regulations. About a month ago I caught him leaving the park with a bucketful of coral in the back of his truck. He tried to tell me the law doesn't apply to Conchs like him, but—"

"Conchs? Aren't they a kind of shell?" Bess asked.

"Around here, a Conch is more than just a shell," Delia said. "It's also a nickname for families who've lived on the Keys since the old wrecking days, back in the seventeen and eighteen hundreds."

She opened the door to the Visitor Center, and we stepped into a big room with an information desk, some displays, and a huge circular tank full of coral and tropical fish. Delia headed for a door marked EMPLOYEES ONLY on the other side of the tank.

"Most of the people who lived here then made a living salvaging cargo from ships that went aground on the reef," she explained. "They got their nickname because they used conch shells like trumpets, blowing into them to announce a wreck."

"So were they pirates?" George asked.

"Sounds kind of like it," Bess reasoned. "They took things that didn't belong to them, right?"

Delia paused next to the tank and thought for a moment. "Not exactly. There *were* pirates who hid out in the mangrove swamps and attacked passing ships. But wreckers were different. They took cargo from sinking ships—stuff that would have been lost at sea if they didn't get it. Then they sold it."

"Maybe Chick thinks of himself as a kind of modern-day wrecker," Bess said. "Except he takes coral from the reef instead of cargo from ships."

"Great, just don't tell that to him. All I need is for Chick to romanticize what he does," Delia said, rolling her eyes. "Every time I think of him taking that coral I get mad all over again."

She glanced at the corals that stuck up from the sand inside the glass tank. Some looked like rocks, while others looked like feathery fans waving in the gentle current. "It's taken over five thousand years for the coral reef to build up. Not to mention that tons of animals depend on the reef for food and protection. Fish, sponges, crabs, turtles, lobsters . . . you name it. That's why it's not legal even to touch the coral, much less take any. Too bad people like Chick don't get how important it is to protect corals and the other special wildlife we have here."

Listening to Delia, I had a pretty good idea of what the trouble was that she had mentioned. "Is that what you need our help with?" I asked. "Stopping Chick from taking coral?"

"Yes," she admitted. "Actually, the problem is even bigger than that. Key Largo's got hundreds of rare plants and animals. Even though they're protected, tourists can't resist taking home a couple of rare orchids or butterflies when they find them. Pennekamp is big, nearly two hundred square miles. So we can't catch every poacher—we just don't have the manpower. But I'd do anything to get people like Chick, the ones who take lots of anything they can get their hands on, and then sell them to collectors."

"Sounds serious," George said. "Especially if Chick is taking more than just coral."

Delia led the way through the EMPLOYEES ONLY door. We entered an area divided into work cubicles, and Delia headed for a desk near the door. Lean-

14

ing against it, she crossed her arms over the front of her parks uniform. "I can't know for sure what he's taking without catching him in the act," she told us. "But I keep seeing him around the park, and I doubt it's because he wants to hike our nature trails or take a snorkeling tour. Last week his truck was parked off the highway next to Pennekamp. When my boss and I hiked into the trees later, we found one that had been stripped clean of butterfly orchids."

"Ouch," Bess said, grimacing. "Let me guess. They're endangered?"

Delia nodded. "There must have been thirty or forty orchids there before, and now they're gone."

"Geez." George shook her head in disgust. "Couldn't you arrest Chick? I mean, you caught him with coral in his truck!"

"It's not that easy," Delia told us. "Chick gave me some story about how the coral came from someplace in Asia and not from here. I'm sure he was lying, but I couldn't prove it—not without catching him in the act. And that can be really hard in a place as big as Pennekamp. That's why I didn't make a big deal of it when I called. I want you to have fun while you're here."

"Hey, what could be more fun than stopping a bad guy from hurting the reef? We'll definitely do whatever we can," I said, turning to Bess and George. "Right?"

15

"Definitely," Bess agreed.

"Especially if checking out the reef is part of our investigation," George added with a grin.

"That can be arranged," Delia promised. Her eyes sparkled with fun as she continued, "In fact, why don't we start right now?" She grabbed a bag from her desk drawer and headed back toward the door. "We might not have enough time to see the reef, but I can give you a tour of the mangrove swamps and beaches. You can see some amazing birds. A couple of the boats at the marina are reserved for parks personnel. We can take one of those."

"Look at that heron!" Bess exclaimed. "Over there, on that channel marker. Isn't it gorgeous?"

We had just set out from the marina and were heading down a wide channel lined by mangroves on both sides. Sure enough, perched on one of its long legs atop the channel marker was a regal-looking snow-white heron.

"Mmm," I agreed. The afternoon sun felt great on my face, the breeze was soft and refreshing, and the water looked unbelievably tempting. I was definitely starting to feel like we were on vacation. Delia kept our boat going slowly, so I reached over the side and let my fingers trail in the warm, salty water. Up ahead, I saw wide-open blue where the channel opened out to the sea. I couldn't help wishing that my boyfriend, Ned Nickerson, could have taken time off college to be here. On the other hand, being away from Ned meant we had more time to get reacquainted with Delia.

"You must love living here," I said, glancing over my sunglasses at her.

"I've gotten used to the tropical life, if that's what you mean," she said. "Here, it's all about the sun and sea. Some of my friends have never seen snow except on TV or in the movies. Everyone's into fishing, swimming, boating, tennis, gardening. . . . My boyfriend lives for scuba diving and snorkeling."

"Boyfriend?" Bess asked, arching an eyebrow.

This was the first I'd heard too about Delia having a boyfriend. It made me realize how much news we had to catch up on.

"His name's Steve," Delia said, blushing a little. "Steve Manning. We've been dating for a few months. He's having dinner with us, so you'll meet him tonight after the *Island Scout* comes in. That's the boat he works on."

George had been looking at the smaller channels that branched off from the main channel and wound among the mangroves. She turned toward Delia and said, "So he's a fisherman?"

"Not exactly. At least, not the kind of fisherman

you mean," Delia answered. "Steve fishes for sunken treasure, not fish."

"Treasure? For real?" Bess asked, her eyes lighting up.

"I think I read about that in that magazine *Wild Explorations*," George said. "You know, about how the coral reefs used to be big trouble for Spanish ships bringing gold from South America. Lots of them sank off the Florida Keys during storms and stuff. Didn't some guy find a treasure that had been sitting at the bottom of the sea since the sixteen hundreds?"

Delia nodded. "That was the treasure from the *Atocha*, a Spanish galleon that sank in 1622. But plenty of other ships went aground on the reef too. A lot of the gold from them has never been recovered," she said.

"Think of it," Bess said dreamily. "Gold coins and goblets and jewels just lying at the bottom of the sea for all these years."

"If you don't mind, I'd rather think about *finding* it," George said.

I could practically see dollar signs in her eyes. Not that George is money hungry or anything, but she's always trying to scrape together enough cash for her next PalmPilot or wireless modem. Not that I could blame her for being tempted. Who *wouldn't* want to discover a sunken treasure?

"You and Steve think exactly alike, George," Delia

said, laughing. "He's signed on to a crew that's been searching for the *Catarina*. That's another Spanish galleon that sank off Key Largo during the big hurricane of 1622. It was carrying a fortune in gold, and Steve figures it's just a matter of time before they find it."

Delia steered our boat around a kayaker who was paddling out of one of the smaller channels. A moment later we cleared the mangrove trees, and Bess looked out at the wide expanse of deep-blue water ahead of us. "What makes them think they can find it after all this time?" she asked.

"For one thing, treasure-hunting equipment gets more sophisticated all the time," Delia told us. "You should see all the stuff they've got on the *Island Scout*. Sonar, radar, metal detectors, digital imaging equipment, computer-generated scatter patterns . . . I can't begin to keep it all straight when Steve tries to—"

She stopped in midsentence and frowned. "That's weird," she murmured, staring at something to our left.

Turning, I saw a sleek-looking red motorboat coming out of the mangroves. At least I *thought* it was coming out. But instead of continuing in our direction, the boat slowed to a stop.

"Is something wrong?" Bess asked, glancing at the boat.

"I'm not sure," Delia said, her eyes still fixed on the other boat. "It's just odd that he stopped when he saw us."

The driver of the red boat was too far away to see clearly. The brim of his baseball cap hid most of his face. All I saw was a blue T-shirt and dark cap. Then, all at once, I heard the buzz-saw sound of the engine revving. The boat spun around in a U-turn and flew back down the tiny channel.

Talk about alarm bells. About a zillion of them went off inside my head. "What's he running from?" I wondered.

"Us. At least I think so. He must have spotted my uniform," Delia said. "And trust me, the only people who run from parks employees are the ones who are up to no good."

Chase Through the Mangroves

I **can't just let** him get away. Hang on, everyone!"

Delia spun the wheel and then hit the gas. The sudden forward surge sent us all flying.

"Whoa!" Bess cried, grabbing the side of our boat as it flew forward.

So much for relaxing. My whole body was on hyperalert mode. I could hear the high-pitched whine of the other boat over the droning of our own motor. As we bounced across the waves, I felt the needle-sharp spray of saltwater on my face. I had to keep wiping my eyes to keep the narrow channel in sight. We entered it just as the red boat fishtailed around a bend in the channel ahead of us.

"He's crazy to go so fast!" George said.

I wasn't about to disagree. The red boat swung

wildly back and forth as it took the turn. Not that we were going much slower. The mangroves were a green and brown blur as we whizzed past.

"There!" Bess cried, as we rounded the first bend.

The boat was farther ahead of us now. We saw a red flash and then it was gone around another corner.

"Come on," Delia said under her breath. She inched the throttle up, and a moment later we flew around the bend.

"Ouch!" I cried, as a branch hit my arm with a stinging slap. We were so close to the tangled mangrove roots that I was sure we were going to—

Bam!

Everything was happening so fast that it took a second to realize it wasn't *our* boat that had hit something. The high-pitched whine of the other engine choked off into silence. We shot around the next bend in time to see the red boat bounce off some mangrove roots like a Ping-Pong ball and then hit the water at an angle.

"It's going to flip over!" Bess cried.

Somehow the guy managed to keep the boat right side up. He had his back to us, working frantically at the controls.

"That's it. We've got him," Delia said, with a triumphant look on her face.

Too bad things didn't work out that way. No

sooner were the words out of Delia's mouth than the engine of the red boat roared back to life. The boat fishtailed into some mangrove roots on the other side of the channel and then flew around a corner. The last thing I saw was a nasty-looking brown scrape on the side of the boat—and a flash of white as something bounced over the stern and into the water.

"Wait—something fell out!" I said. "It looks like a plastic bag."

I could see the indecision on Delia's face. For a second I thought she might keep going after the boat. But then she pulled back on the throttle, and we slowed down sharply. By the time George reached over and grabbed the bulging bag from the water, all we heard of the other boat was a faint whine in the distance.

"Take a look," George said, holding the bag out. "Orchids. Tons of them!"

"Butterfly orchids," Delia said, taking one and gently fingering its waxy leaves.

I had seen orchids from the florist before. But the ones in the bag were totally different. I could see how they'd gotten their name. They had the same coloring as a monarch butterfly—a rich yellow-orange and mottled brown. There were at least a dozen of them in the bag, and a few more lay floating on the water.

"Again?" Bess asked, looking at Delia in surprise. "That's the same kind you think Chick Russell took that other time, right? So that means it was him we were chasing!"

"Chick was wearing a black baseball cap, like the guy in the boat," I said, thinking it out. "But Chick's T-shirt was orange, not blue."

"So maybe this was someone else," Delia said. She gazed ahead down the mangrove-lined channel. "Chick drives a beat-up truck that's about a million years old. I doubt he has the money to buy a fancy new boat like that red one. Still, it would be just like him to do something like this. Whoever that was probably moored the boat in the mangroves and then hiked to the spots where butterfly orchids grow. There aren't that many places on Key Largo where they grow in the wild, but a local like Chick might know where to look."

I made a mental note to find out more about Chick Russell.

"Do you think we could figure out where the orchids came from?" I asked Delia as she placed the bag of orchids at her feet. "Maybe whoever took them left some kind of clue there."

"We could try," she said, with a shrug. "Actually, a couple of botanists are coming down from Tallahassee tomorrow. They've been keeping track of endangered plants, and I promised to show them some of our rarer species. Why don't you come along, and we'll see what we find?"

With that, she put the boat back in gear and turned it slowly around. "I know I promised you a tour, but we'd better head back so I can report this to my boss."

We were pretty quiet during the trip back. I looked around the marina after we docked, but I didn't see any red boat. Not that I'd expected to. I didn't think the guy who'd taken those orchids would be dumb enough to leave his boat anywhere in the state park.

Delia said we'd probably find her boss in the greenhouse, a glass structure that was tucked away among some palms and oaks beyond a camping area. The second we stepped inside, a blanket of steamy air wrapped itself around us.

At first I saw only dense, lush greenery and a slew of colorful flowers that I couldn't even begin to name. Then I spotted a woman through one of the glass doors. She wore a paint-smudged apron over her clothes and stood next to an easel with a paintbrush in her hand. Her graying blond hair was pulled back into a twist that made her high cheekbones stand out.

"That's your boss?" Bess said, nodding at the woman.

"No. Mr. Rinaldi wears a uniform, like me," Delia explained. "That's—"

"Delia! Hello, darling!" the woman gushed, before Delia could finish. She waved her paintbrush, and I saw that the tip of it glistened with purple paint.

"My dear, you must tell me when you and Steve are coming for dinner. I tried to get him to set a date, but you know how men are. You would think he'd find time to see his own mother, but he simply won't commit. . . ."

So this was Steve Manning's mother. She had a dramatic flair — that was for sure. She was really playing up the unappreciated mother role, but Delia was too distracted to take much notice. Her eyes darted around the greenhouse.

"Um, sure, Mrs. Manning," Delia said. "Is Mr. Rinaldi around?"

"Nick? Why, I think he's—" Mrs. Manning broke off suddenly, then exclaimed, "My goodness! Are those butterfly orchids?"

She couldn't get over to Delia fast enough. Plucking one of the orchids from the bag, she held it up and examined it closely. A dreamy expression came over her face. "Lovely . . . just lovely. Wherever did you get them?" she asked.

When we told her, Mrs. Manning pressed her lips together disapprovingly. "Poaching . . . how awful!" she said. "Still, I suppose nature's loss is my gain. There'll be more orchids for me to paint now."

"Talk about self-centered . . . ," Bess whispered to me.

And how! Mrs. Manning didn't even seem to

notice how distraught Delia was. "You *will* be adding them to the collection of lovelies here, won't you?" Steve's mother rambled on blithely. She gestured to a long table next to her easel, and I saw that dozens of orchids grew in pots there. The "lovelies," as Mrs. Manning called them, were in rich shades of violet, white, yellow, orange, red, purple, and even bluish black. Each one was like a waxy tropical gem.

"My boss lets Mrs. Manning come here to paint," Delia told us. She nodded at the canvas on Mrs. Manning's easel, which was filled with the half-painted image of a fuchsia orchid that was a perfect replica of a real one growing in a pot on the table. "But the real point of the greenhouse is to cultivate rare species from this area so that if a bad storm wipes out some plant . . ."

"Or if someone steals them," George put in, nodding at the bag of orchids Delia held.

"That, too," Delia agreed. "Anyway, if something bad happens, we can use the plants we have here to reintroduce the species to nature. So we probably will add these orchids to the ones that are here already, like Mrs. Manning said."

"And such marvelous examples, too," Mrs. Manning went on gleefully. As she gazed at the orchids, a greedy gleam came into her eyes.

"It's rare to find butterfly orchids in the wild. Quite rare!" she said. "I'd kill to get a few of my own."

4

Orchid Envy

Bess, George, and I all did a double take when we heard that.

"Excuse me? What did you say?" Bess asked.

Mrs. Manning gave a quick laugh. "It's just a figure of speech, my dear. I'm afraid I haven't had much luck growing orchids myself. That's why I come here to paint them."

She bent closer to Delia and gave a hopeful smile. "You do have quite a few of these. Surely you can spare just one?" she asked.

"Is she for real?" George whispered, rolling her eyes.

At least Delia didn't let the older woman push her around. "You know I can't, Mrs. Manning. It's against the law," she said firmly. Her eyes flickered to more distant parts of the greenhouse. "Oh! There's Mr. Rinaldi. . . . I'll have to take that back now."

She pried the butterfly orchid from Mrs. Manning's grasp, then headed toward a doorway at the far end of the glassed-in room. Barely visible among the leafy trees and vines was a dark-haired man whose parks uniform blended perfectly with the surrounding greenery.

"I thought we'd never get away," Delia said under her breath. "Steve's mother is nice, but she's kind of . . ."

"Self-centered?" Bess offered. "Greedy? Overdramatic?"

"I knew you'd understand," Delia said, chuckling.

George glanced back over her shoulder at Mrs. Manning. "Did you see the way she was all over those orchids? Makes you wonder, doesn't it?"

Delia blinked in surprise, pausing in midstep. "You mean, about her being the poacher? I really doubt it," she said. "Sure, she's a little self-involved. . . ."

"A little?" George asked, raising an eyebrow.

"All right, a lot," Delia admitted. "But I can't picture her tromping through mangroves to steal orchids. Anyway, the person in that boat was a guy, remember?"

She had a point. And she definitely knew Steve's mother better than we did. But Mrs. Manning's attitude still bugged me.

As we entered the back room of the greenhouse, I saw that Delia's boss was using a hand rake to work the soil at the roots of a small tree. When he saw Delia, he straightened up and smiled.

"Didn't I just give you the afternoon off?" he asked. Then his gaze landed on the bag of orchids. "Uh-oh, don't tell me . . ."

He looked anything but happy when Delia told him what had happened. "Looks like our orchid poacher has struck again," he said, running a hand through his hair. Then he turned to Bess and George and me and said, "You must be the friends Delia's been telling me about. I'm Nick Rinaldi, the head biological scientist here at Pennekamp. Sorry your visit had to start with trouble."

There was something straightforward and likable about Delia's boss. "I just wish we'd caught the guy who took these," I told him, nodding at the bag of orchids.

"Well, we got the orchids back, anyway," he said.

That didn't make me feel much better. Dad says I have a stubborn streak a mile wide, but I prefer to call it determination. Whatever it is, it kicked in full force when I thought about the guy in the red boat. Getting the orchids back wasn't enough. I wanted to stop whoever had taken them from poaching orchids—or anything else—ever again.

After giving the butterfly orchids to Mr. Rinaldi, we left the coral reef state park and drove to Delia's. She lived farther down the island, on a small road off of Route 1. Following her in our rental car, we snaked past pines, oaks, and palm trees and wound up at a small, pale green stucco house across from a marina. White pebbles surrounded the house, and they crunched under our sandals as we walked.

"This is Rock Harbor," Delia said, gesturing to the covelike circle of water across the street. Docks, houses, restaurants, palm trees, and a local fishery lined the harbor. A few boats were coming in for the day. Delia brightened when she spotted a white boat about thirty feet long that was puttering toward one of the docks.

"Hey! We're in luck. The *Island Scout* is just coming in for the day," she said.

"The boat Steve goes treasure hunting on?" George shaded her eyes and gazed toward the marina. "Can we see it?"

"Sure. I want you to meet Steve and the Salazars. Diego and Lucy are the ones who hired Steve to help search for the *Catarina*. The *Island Scout* is their boat," Delia said.

After running our bags inside, we ran to the dock. A deeply tanned man with a stocky, muscular build stood outside the boat's small cabin. He wore swim trunks and a tennis visor and was busy with a heavy rope that lay coiled on the deck at the front of the boat. Judging by his graying hair, I figured he was one of the Salazars and not Delia's boyfriend.

"You're just in time to help, Delia!" he called out, holding up a looped end of rope. "Tie us up, will you?"

"Sure thing, Diego." Delia caught the rope and slipped the loop over the top of the mooring post. Then she did the same with a rope he threw from the stern of the boat. Just as she finished, a woman wearing a wet suit stepped out of the cabin. Her still-damp dark hair was pulled back into a ponytail, and tiny wrinkles showed at the corners of her eyes and mouth when she smiled at Delia.

"Hey, Lucy," Delia greeted her. "Where's Steve?"

"You got me," Mrs. Salazar answered, shrugging. "He didn't come today. Called this morning to say he had a doctor's appointment."

Delia frowned slightly. "He didn't say anything about it to me. I hope he can still make it for dinner," she said. "He's supposed to meet us at seven."

"Which means you still have"—Diego checked his watch, then grinned at us—"one hour for Lucy and me to give your friends the grand tour of the *Island Scout*." Turning to Bess and George and me, he bowed slightly. "Diego Salazar at your service, ladies. Would you like to come aboard?"

"We'd love to!" George said right away.

The three of us introduced ourselves, and before we knew it, we were scrambling on board. As we followed the Salazars to the cabin, Delia said, "You guys are going to love this. The *Scout* may not look like anything special on the outside, but on the inside . . ."

"Wow . . . it's awesome!" Bess exclaimed, stepping through the door ahead of George and me.

I had to agree. The inside of the cabin looked more like a mission control center than part of a boat. One whole wall was lined with computers, screens, charts, keyboards, and control panels. Other kinds of equipment were hanging from the walls, and charts and notebooks were piled on the table. I didn't know what most of the stuff was, but George looked right at home.

"Digital imaging equipment, radar, sonar, two computers," she said, pointing to the various machines. "Impressive!"

"We like to think so," Diego said proudly. He went over to a computer and tapped a couple of keys. Immediately, a map of the ocean floor appeared, with lines of longitude and latitude marked. "We have software that helps us to predict how the cargo of the *Catarina* might have scattered when the ship hit the reef."

"Keep it under your hats, but we think we're getting closer," Lucy added. "Take a look at what we found today."

She lifted a sealed plastic bag from a bucket that sat on the floor near the table. Inside, surrounded by seawater, were two ancient-looking golden disks about two inches in diameter. Some kind of white deposit had corroded them, but I could see a cross and a bunch of letters stamped into the gold.

"Are those coins?" I asked.

"Seventeenth-century gold doubloons from Mexico," Lucy said, nodding. "Diego and I are pretty sure they were part of the *Catarina's* cargo."

Bess's eyes went wide as she stared at the coins. "Then you *must* be close to finding the wreck of the *Catarina*," she said.

"And the treasure," George added.

"Wait till Steve hears," Delia said, grinning. "He'll go crazy!"

The Salazars' enthusiasm was definitely rubbing off. We all started firing questions at Diego and Lucy, until Diego finally threw up his hands and said, "Why don't you girls come with us tomorrow and see for yourselves how our little treasure-hunting operation works? Who knows? Maybe you'll be on hand for the big find."

"Sounds great!" George said. She turned to Bess, Delia, and me. "Let's do it."

"Um, you guys go without me," Delia said, hesitating. "I've got to meet those botanists from Tallahassee tomorrow. Plus, I want to do a little scouting around."

Bess's hand flew to her mouth. "About the orchids! How could we forget?" she said. "We definitely want to help with that."

"Absolutely," I agreed.

George had moved over to one of the computer screens and was asking Diego and Lucy about the software program they used. I was pretty sure she hadn't heard Bess.

"George?" Bess started toward her cousin, but Delia stopped her.

"Don't worry about it," Delia said. "You guys shouldn't miss out on the chance to find the *Catarina*'s treasure. I'll be fine on my own, really."

As tempting as it was to go out on the *Scout*, I knew I'd be distracted the whole time, thinking about the person who had poached those orchids. "I'd rather stick around here and see what we can find out about Chick Russell and that red boat," I said.

"Me too. We're in this together, right, George?" Bess said, touching George's arm. "Maybe we can take a rain check."

George looked at Bess as if she had just suggested jumping into a pool of hot lava. "Are you crazy? If they found doubloons today, tomorrow could be the day they find the mother lode! We can't miss that," she said.

"A promise is a promise," Bess shot back. "Anyway, what's more important? Finding some old ship, or helping a friend?"

George opened her mouth to say something, but I guess she changed her mind. Clamping it shut again, she turned and walked to the other end of the cabin.

"George?" Bess persisted.

But George had bent over a pile of metal detectors and didn't answer.

5

Cousin Trouble

"I'll tell you what," Lucy said pleasantly. "We'll leave the offer open, and if any of you want to join us, just meet us here tomorrow morning at seven, okay?"

I could tell she had sized up the situation and wanted to give us a chance to work out our differences later, in private. Seemed like a good idea, since we weren't getting anywhere at the moment.

"Thanks," Delia told her. "We should really get going. We have to meet Steve soon."

We carried our bags up the outside stairs to Delia's second-floor apartment. None of us said a word until after we were inside.

"Nice place," I said, putting my bag down next to the door. I glanced around the cozy kitchen area and living room. Sliding glass doors led to a balcony that faced the marina.

"Um, Delia, about tomorrow . . . ," George began.

"You should go with the Salazars," Delia said. "I don't want you to miss out on finding the *Catarina*."

"Really? You're sure?" George asked. "I mean, we *did* come here to help you."

"It's just one day," Delia said. She led the way down a small hall to a spare room with a foldout bed and two cots in it. "We have the whole rest of the week to look for the guy who took those orchids."

"Besides, Bess and Delia and I will be working on it until you get back," I added.

Smiling, George leaned against the wall. "Well, then I guess I will go," she said. "Thanks, guys."

Something told me that wasn't the decision Bess was hoping for. Without looking at George, she dropped her bag on one of the cots. I didn't miss the frown that darkened her face. But she must have decided not to fight about it anymore. Opening her suitcase, she stood back and surveyed the contents that were jammed inside.

"Time to move on to the next big question," she said. "What should we wear?"

"Clothes?" George cracked.

Bess cocked her head toward George and rolled

her eyes. "Hardee har." She went back to rummaging through her suitcase.

Things were back to normal—for the moment, anyway. Not that we should have worried about getting ready on time. By seven thirty, Steve still hadn't gotten to Delia's. We were working on our second round of iced tea on the balcony when a white hatchback pulled up behind Delia's car.

"Finally!" Delia said. Jumping up from her chair, she went to the railing and waved.

The guy who got out had short blond hair and the same high cheekbones as Mrs. Manning. It was easy to see that he was her son. He grinned up at us with a grimy, sweat-drenched face. Dirt and perspiration stains covered his blue T-shirt and jeans, too.

"You're late—and we're famished!" Delia called down to him. "Where've you been?"

"I'll tell you in a sec," he called back. "I just have to get changed."

Delia stared after him as he grabbed a sports bag from the backseat and jogged toward the *Island Scout*. "What was he doing at that doctor's office? Mud wrestling?" she asked.

I was wondering the same thing. Luckily, when Steve came back his face was clean and he was wearing crisp khakis and a button-down shirt. He plunked down a gym bag and said, "Good thing I always keep some extra clothes on the boat. Sorry you had to wait."

He looked at George, me, and Bess in turn. "Let me guess. You must be George. You're Nancy, and you're Bess."

"Pretty good! How'd you know?" Bess said, with an impressed nod.

"It wasn't too hard," Steve said, pouring himself a glass of iced tea. "Delia showed me your pictures in the River Heights High yearbook."

"No wonder!" I said, laughing. "Now let's see if we can make a guess about you."

"Okay. Shoot," Steve said.

"Well . . ." I nodded at his sports bag and said, "Based on how you looked when you drove up, I'd guess that your doctor recommended a treatment of extremely physical outdoor exercise."

Steve stared at me blankly.

"The Salazars told us you had to miss work for a doctor's appointment?" Delia prompted him.

"Oh—yeah." Steve shifted nervously in his deck chair. Then the corners of his mouth curved up in a sheepish smile and he said, "Okay, you caught me. I didn't have any appointment. I just needed a break from Lucy and Diego, that's all."

"*Now?*" George said, gaping at him. "When they're so close to finding the *Catarina*?"

We told Steve about the doubloons the Salazars had found. I thought he'd be excited, the way everyone else had been. But Steve just rolled his eyes. "It's not the first time we've found a few coins," he told us. "They might not be anywhere near the mother lode from the *Catarina*. It's been almost four hundred years since she went down. The coins could've scattered miles from the rest of the gold."

"But Lucy and Diego were so excited," Delia said, looking confused.

"They've been excited before, but nothing big has ever turned up," Steve said bitterly. "I'm starting to think I'm just wasting my time going out on the *Scout* every day. That's why I called in sick today. I need some time to think about whether I want to keep diving for Diego and Lucy."

I wasn't sure what to make of that. I didn't think lying to the Salazars was the best way to handle the situation. Besides which, Steve hadn't even bothered to call Delia to tell her he'd be late to meet us. Still, I didn't want to get overly critical when I didn't even know him yet.

We were all hungry, so we headed out to the restaurant. The place Delia had in mind was called Gaby's Seafood Grille, overlooking the water right next to the marina. As we walked there from her house, the yummy smells of fried fish made me even hungrier.

"So, Steve, you never did tell us what you were up to today," Delia said. "What were you doing that you had to make us wait till we're practically starved?"

She was teasing, but her words made Steve tighten up like a metal spring that was ready to pop. "Um, nothing special. I was just out and about," he said. "Guess I lost track of the time."

"For the whole day?" Delia pressed.

"Mmm," he said vaguely. He tugged at his collar, and I got the definite feeling Delia's questions were making him uncomfortable. A nagging voice in the back of my head told me I was missing something. It wasn't until Steve and Delia walked into the restaurant ahead of us that it hit me.

"Guys!" I said, stopping Bess and George outside the door. "Did you notice the color of Steve's T-shirt—the one he had on before he changed?"

It took them a second. But then they both yelled, "Blue!"

"Just like the guy who poached the orchids," I said. "He might not be the guy we saw. But don't you think it's weird that Steve won't say where he was today?"

George nodded. "Tromping around stealing orchids could make a guy pretty sweaty," she commented. "No wonder he doesn't want to talk about it."

"Poor Delia!" Bess said sympathetically.

I couldn't imagine how I'd feel if Ned did anything like that. "Maybe there's some other reason he's acting weird," I said, as much to myself as to Bess and George. "But we should definitely find out more."

We went inside and found Delia and Steve at a table on the back porch, overlooking the marina. The view was amazing, complete with rose-tinted clouds, fishing boats coming in to dock for the night, and palm trees swaying in the breeze with the setting sun behind them. As we sat down, I realized that Delia was telling Steve about the poached orchids.

"So we chased the guy, but he got away," she was saying. "I just hope we can catch the guy before he poaches something else."

Steve kept his cool. "Good luck," he said.

Bess, George, and I all watched Steve as if he were a specimen under a microscope. As our waiter brought us menus, Bess turned to Steve and asked, "Did you happen to visit Pennekamp today? Maybe you went boating that way when you were 'out and about'?"

"Did you?" Delia's face was full of hope as she turned to her boyfriend. "Maybe you saw the guy who took the orchids! He was driving a brand-new boat. A sleek thing. Bright red."

"Red?" Steve repeated. For a second, he looked kind of shell-shocked, like a bomb had just gone off under his chair. Then he shook his head and said, "Actually, I never made it anywhere near the park. Sorry."

I didn't miss the nervous flicker in his eyes, or the tight set to his jaw. They made me more certain than ever that Steve was hiding something.

"You think *Steve* took those orchids from Pennekamp?" Delia asked. She flopped back on her couch, shaking her head back and forth. "No way. He wouldn't."

It was almost eleven, and Bess, George, Delia, and I were lounging in Delia's living room in our pj's. Steve had driven home after dinner, so we'd finally had a chance to talk to Delia about him.

Not that it was easy.

"We could be wrong," I said. "But Steve acted . . . well, like he wasn't being totally honest."

"Look, I'll admit Steve was acting weird tonight," she said. "He's got a lot on his mind. But whatever's going on, I'm sure it's not illegal. He'll tell me about it when he's ready."

I hoped she was right, but when we went to sleep I still had my doubts. I kept wondering why Steve would hide something from his own girlfriend—and what we could do to help Delia catch whoever had poached those orchids.

I'm not sure how much sleep I got. But it definitely felt too early when the electronic beep in George's watch woke me up the next morning. "Huh?" I mumbled.

"Turn that thing off! It's only six o'clock," I heard Bess grumble in the semidarkness. She rolled over and stuffed her pillow on top of her head.

I must have fallen back asleep too, because when I opened my eyes again, bright sunshine flooded our room and Bess was getting dressed.

"Wake up, sleepyhead. Everyone's gone!" she said, pulling an embroidered blouse over her jeans skirt.

"Hmmm?" I mumbled, yawning.

"I heard Delia's car pull out a few minutes ago. That's what woke me up," Bess told me. "George must have left to meet the Salazars hours ago."

It took me a second to remember that George had gone out on the *Island Scout*. And that Bess and I were supposed to help Delia find the orchid poacher. "Why didn't Delia wake us?" I asked, jumping out of bed.

"Relax. She left us a note."

Bess handed me a sheet of paper with a message scrawled across it:

Have some paperwork to take care of at Pennekamp. Botanists from Tallahassee

45

arriving at noon. Why don't you two check out
the sights and meet me at my office then?

"Delia left these, too." Bess picked up a wad of
tourist pamphlets and brochures from her cot. She
took one from the top and waved it under my nose.
"I definitely think we should check out this place."

"The Key Largo Flea Market?" I said, taking the
pamphlet. "Looks like fun. But wouldn't you rather
see what we can find out about Chick Russell? Delia
must have a phone book around here. Maybe we can
find out where he lives."

"Or maybe we don't have to. Take a look at the list
of vendors," Bess said.

Opening the pamphlet, I saw that dozens of vendors were listed. They sold everything from clothing
and jewelry to shells, antiques, and nautical clocks.
Two-thirds of the way down the list, I saw Chick
Russell's name.

"It says here he sells shells and local memorabilia,"
I said, lowering the pamphlet to grin at Bess. "Well,
we can't go home without a few souvenirs, can we?"

"Now you're talking. The flea market is pretty
close to Pennekamp, too, at Mile Marker 103.5," Bess
said. She lifted a teasing eyebrow. "Think you can
find it?"

"Very funny," I said. Actually, finding our way

46

around Key Largo wasn't complicated once we figured out that everyone used the mile markers along Route 1 as landmarks. Pennekamp was at Mile Marker 102.5. The turnoff to get to Delia's was farther down the island, at Mile Marker 99.5. Delia had told us the miles counted down along the keys, with the zero point at Key West, the last island in the chain. Key Largo was pretty narrow, so most businesses were on or near Route 1. Getting to the flea market was a breeze, even for me. Before long we were parking near a long, low building on the bayside of Route 1. Open-air booths were lined up along the outside edge of the building, and their colorful, tented canopies gave the place the look of a festive fairgrounds. A woman at the first booth we came to was selling funny little figurines made from shells. Through the open doors, I saw dozens more vendors set up inside.

"Keep your eyes peeled for an information booth," I said. "Maybe someone there can tell us where to find Chick."

We were just about to head inside when I heard someone say, "You won't find finer examples in all of Key Largo, ma'am. I guarantee it."

The familiar drawling tone made me stop short. Sure enough, when I turned I saw Chick Russell standing at a booth about twenty feet away.

"Bingo," I said.

A customer blocked part of the booth, so at first all I could see were some fan-shaped corals and a pile of shells on the display counter. Once the person moved, I caught a glimpse of a tigerlike yellow and brown flower with graceful green leaves.

"Butterfly orchids," I breathed. "Bess, he's selling *butterfly orchids*."

6

A Slippery Suspect

That's not all," said Bess. "Did you see who's trying to buy one from him?"

Until that moment, all my attention had been focused on Chick. But as Bess and I walked over, I recognized the blond twist and high cheekbones of the person standing in front of his booth.

"Mrs. Manning," I said, rolling my eyes. "That figures."

Steve's mother held up a pot containing a butterfly orchid. Half a dozen others sat on the display table in front of her.

"I guess she didn't want to take no for an answer when Delia wouldn't give her one yesterday," Bess said under her breath. She walked up to Mrs. Manning and tapped her arm. "You're not going to buy that, are you?" she said, nodding at the orchid.

"Excuse me?" Mrs. Manning lowered the flower and looked at us in surprise. "Ah! Delia's friends," she said. "How lovely to see you. But . . . I think I must have heard you wrong. Did you say I *shouldn't* buy this lovely orchid?"

"I wouldn't if I were you," I told her. "It might have been poached."

Chick Russell had been standing behind the booth just watching us. He wore the same black Florida Marlins baseball cap he'd had on the day before, and earphones that were plugged into a silver digital music player that peeked out from his shirt pocket. Apparently he could still hear us, because he turned a wide smile on Mrs. Manning and said, "I can assure you that these are totally legitimate, ma'am. My cousin grows them at his place up in Sarasota."

Glancing at Bess and me, he added, "I'm sure these ladies have good intentions, but I think you'll agree that they can't possibly know more about my business than I do myself."

He was a smooth talker, all right. Mrs. Manning seemed totally satisfied with his explanation, but I had a feeling she'd be happy with *any* excuse to walk away with that butterfly orchid.

"Do you have your cousin's business card?" I spoke

up. "If they really weren't stolen, maybe I'll buy some butterfly orchids myself."

Chick made a big show of patting his pockets. "Gee, I must have given my last one away. Sorry," he said. He acted so insincere that even Mrs. Manning seemed to notice. With a sigh, she put the butterfly orchid back down on Chick's display counter.

"Well . . . I suppose if I can't be absolutely certain, I'd better not buy one," she said regretfully.

Bess shot a triumphant smile at me, but Chick seemed anything but pleased. As Steve's mother moved through the doorway to the flea market booths inside, his smooth smile disappeared.

"Do you always chase off other people's paying customers?" he asked, as his eyes lingered on mine. "Hey—you're that girl I saw at Pennekamp yesterday. Delia Duke's friend. Did you give her my message?"

I couldn't believe it when he flashed me one of his cocky smiles. Was this guy for real? The day before he'd bragged that Delia couldn't stop him from doing what he wanted. He'd practically admitted to poaching. Yet here he was claiming to be a legitimate businessman.

"Can you honestly tell us that these orchids weren't poached?" I asked.

"They had to be," Bess piped up. "Just like the corals Delia caught you with in your truck."

Chick winked at us as he adjusted the sound on his digital music player. "That's quite an accusation, but I seriously doubt you can prove it."

I don't get rattled very easily, but there was something in his eyes—a taunting gleam—that really irked me. Chick obviously didn't think Bess and I were up to the challenge.

I nodded at the fan corals that were lined up on his table. "What about those?" I asked. "If they're not poached, then where'd you get them?"

Chick just shrugged and said, "Florida doesn't have the only coral reef on the planet. These are from the Philippines. If you don't believe me, just ask Kenny DuPris, over at the Shell Emporium."

"Shell Emporium?" I repeated.

But Chick was already turning on the charm to another visitor. Ignoring us, he picked up one of the potted butterfly orchids to show the man.

"*Oooh!* He's doing that on purpose, just to make us mad," Bess fumed.

I had a feeling she was right, but it wasn't like we could do anything to stop him. Plus, I didn't want to give Chick the satisfaction of knowing how well he'd succeeded in getting under our skin.

"We're not going to get any straight answers out of him. Let's go," I said, heading toward the indoor part of the flea market. "Maybe someone in here knows what the Shell Emporium is. Anyway, we still have to find souvenirs to bring back home, remember?"

It turned out that the Shell Emporium was just what it sounded like—a sprawling place where they sold every kind of shell and seaside memorabilia imaginable. Inside and out, there were buckets of shells, corals, and sand dollars, and shelves lined with sponges, funky fish skeletons, shell jewelry, quirky figurines made of shells, shell picture frames . . . you name it. Bess picked up a bracelet for her little sister, Maggie. I almost bought this cool-looking blowfish skeleton for Ned, but then I decided on a shark's-tooth necklace instead. At the register we found Kenny DuPris, the owner.

"I'm surprised to see so much coral here," I said, as he rang up our things. "Since it's illegal to take coral from the reef, I mean."

Kenny had a round, sunburned face, a T-shirt that read "I ♥ SHELL EMPORIUM," and a calm, easygoing way about him. He didn't seem at all taken aback by my comment.

"People come looking for a souvenir from the reef, and we're not about to disappoint them," he told us. "We've got the best supply of shells and corals anywhere on the keys, but most of them aren't from here. All the corals are flown in from the Philippines."

So Chick hadn't been lying about that. I have to admit I was surprised.

"Do you ever sell corals to other vendors?" Bess asked. "Like Chick Russell? He's selling corals at the flea market, and he says they come from you."

Kenny chuckled as he put our things in a bag and pushed it across the counter. "If he says so, I guess it must be true," he said.

"Wait. Are you saying he *doesn't* get corals from you?" I asked, before he could turn to the next customer.

Kenny glanced at the teenage girl who stood in line behind us with her mother. "I sell Chick corals whenever he can scrape a few bucks together. That's about all there is to say about it."

"What about the ones he has now? They look like giant fans. Did you sell those to him?" Bess pressed him.

The woman behind us tapped her foot impatiently. "I really don't remember," Kenny said. "Now, if you'll excuse me . . ."

The woman and her daughter practically pushed us out of the way, so we thanked Kenny and left.

"Did you get the feeling that he was covering for Chick?" Bess asked, as we headed back out to the car.

I nodded. "Too bad we don't have any way of proving it. But maybe we *can* dig up some more information on Chick."

I pulled a scrap of paper from the back pocket of my shorts and showed it to Bess.

"Chick's address?" she guessed.

"I got it from the phone book at Delia's. Feel like taking a detour before we head over to Pennekamp to meet her?"

Bess put her sunglasses on and grinned at me. "Sure. Why not?" she agreed. "Lead the way, Sherlock."

The address I'd written down was on the bayside of Key Largo. We turned off of Route 1 at Mile Marker 102 and found ourselves at the Pelican Bay Trailer Park. Parked among the pitch pines, palms, mimosas, and mosquitoes were a few dozen motor homes. A gravel road wound past them to the water's edge, where a row of houseboats was moored. I guess the heat kept most people inside. We had to knock on a couple of doors before a young woman pointed the way to Chick's place—a white houseboat with a blue tarp tied over its roof.

"Um, Nancy?" Bess said, glancing nervously around as I stepped onto the boat's rear deck. "Breaking and entering was illegal last time I checked."

I moved past a plastic table and chairs and pressed my face against the Plexiglas door. "I'm not actually going inside—just taking a look around."

"Great. Pardon me if I don't exactly find that reassuring," she said.

The sun was sizzling hot on my back. It poured through the windows of Chick's boat, lighting up a messy living area and galley—the boat's tiny kitchen. Clothes, glasses, and tools lay scattered across the couch and half covered a compact stereo and speakers on the table. Empty cans of food and dirty dishes were piled in the sink and on the counter.

"Well, I don't see any butterfly orchids . . . or corals," I said, swatting at a couple of mosquitoes.

"No surprise there. He's got them all at the flea market," Bess pointed out. "What about . . . I don't know, tools or something he could be using to poach things? See anything like that?"

I glanced at Bess over my shoulder. "Like a slick red motorboat?" I suggested.

"Now you're talking." I guess Bess's curiosity was stronger than her fear, because she stepped onto the deck and made her way around the cabin to the other side of the boat. "Well, there *is* a boat here," I heard her say.

When I caught up to her, I understood why she didn't sound more excited. The motorboat that was tied to the back of Chick's houseboat was smaller than the one we'd chased—and much more rundown. It wasn't red, either, but a bleached-out bluish green that looked as if it had sat through more than a few summers baking in the Florida sun.

"It's definitely not the boat the poacher used yesterday," I said.

"But Chick acted so . . . so cocky. Like he was just betting we won't be able to catch him. He's *got* to be the guy we chased," Bess insisted.

I knew exactly how she felt. It was frustrating to come up empty-handed after a whole morning of checking Chick out. I didn't like the bitter taste it left in my mouth, but I wasn't about to give up.

7

Clue in the Cactus

Delia, I had no idea you were going to show us such a wild time. And I do mean *wild*," Bess said.

Delia laughed as she climbed onto a muddy mangrove root and pushed through a dense mass of branches. "Well, you have to get off the beaten path to find the rarer plants on Key Largo," she said.

The two botanists who were visiting from Tallahassee, Florida's capital city, were with us too. Bess and I had hooked up with them at Delia's office right on schedule, at noon. After eating some sandwiches and soda at the park's concession stand, we'd all headed off in Delia's car. The place where she'd parked—next to a wall of trees along Route 1—hadn't looked like anything special. But once we hiked into the trees, we found ourselves in a thick jungle that seemed a world away from the boutiques and restaurants and dive shops of the busier part of Key Largo.

"Believe it or not, Amira and I have never seen some of the plants we'll be looking at today," commented one of the visiting botanists, a tall, lanky guy named Dylan Sherman. "A lot of species migrated here from the Bahamas and aren't found much farther north. Like the Guiana plum, milkbark, and inkwood trees."

The other botanist, Amira Lambo, slapped at the mosquitoes that buzzed relentlessly around us as we made our way through the mangroves behind Delia. "We can't visit every spot where rare and endangered species grow, so we rely on information from people like Delia, who are onsite," Amira said. "This is actually our first time here in Key Largo, even though we've been mapping hot spots for endangered species for months now."

"Most of the rarest and most beautiful plants and animals live in the hardwood hammocks," Delia told us over her shoulder. "Those are places that are higher and drier than the areas surrounding them. They're like little islands hidden away all over Key Largo. Most people don't even know where they are."

"No wonder. You have to be a top athlete just to get there," Bess said. Huffing, she grabbed hold of a branch to help her over the mangrove roots. "Having a mosquito-proof force field wouldn't hurt either. Besides which, I'm totally lost. I couldn't find my way back to your car if my life depended on it!"

"Not to worry. I know where we are," Delia said, laughing.

I was glad *someone* did. Before coming to the mangroves, we'd tromped across craggy limestone dotted with tough-looking, thorny shrubs. Amira and Dylan told us they were called Christmas berry. Those bushes were out of sight behind the mangroves now, and all I saw ahead of us was a dense wall of green and brown.

All of a sudden Delia called out, "We're here. Come on, everyone!"

Bess and I scrambled over the muddy roots behind Amira and Dylan. Soon the mangroves ended, and the swampy mud gave way to drier ground overgrown with an amazingly lush collection of trees, shrubs, grasses, and vines.

"Whoa," Dylan said, stepping around a tree with dark, ridged bark and small green flowers. "Let's see . . . West Indian mahogany, lignum vitae, saffron plum, wild dilly, mahogany mistletoe . . ."

The names were so unfamiliar to me that it was like listening to a foreign language. Dylan and Amira pulled clipboards from their backpacks and took notes as they pointed at different shrubs and trees. But I was on the lookout for something they hadn't spotted yet.

"Hey, Delia, do butterfly orchids grow here?" I asked.

"Sure. A few other rare orchids, too," she said. She pointed at a tree half a dozen feet in front of me. "See those pretty little green-and-brown ones, with the cream-colored center? Those are dollar orchids."

I had never seen orchids in the wild before, and they were truly amazing. Their graceful stems rose from a base of leaves that clung to the bark of the tree. Tufts of flowers rested in every little nook and cranny, covering much of the branches and tree trunk.

"They're gorgeous!" said Bess, coming over for a closer look.

"There are a couple of trees over this way that are usually loaded with butterfly orchids," Delia went on. She circled around an enormous cactus that Dylan and Amira were exclaiming over. The long, prickly stalks were so huge that they hid her from view, but all of a sudden I heard her gasp.

"Oh, no!" came her horrified voice. "I was afraid of this. . . ."

Bess and I took one look at each other and ran over to her. "What! What is it?" Bess asked.

"See that gumbo-limbo tree?" Delia said, pointing to a tree with peeling bark. "It used to be covered with butterfly orchids."

My heart sank when I looked at the tree. Now its branches were completely bare, except for a lone yellow and brown butterfly orchid that rose from a bent limb above our heads. When I moved closer, I saw cut marks on the branches and trunk of the tree.

"I guess now we know where the guy we chased yesterday got those orchids," I said, fingering one of the shallow, moist cuts. "These look pretty fresh."

"But . . . how could anyone know where to find this place?" Amira wondered, looking around in amazement.

"The guy we saw yesterday was in a boat. Delia, didn't you say there's a way to get here from the water?" Bess asked.

Delia gestured vaguely in the opposite direction from the way we'd come. "The ocean's just a couple hundred feet that way," she said. "There's no path, but someone who knows the area could have tied a boat to the mangroves and made his way here."

"Someone like Chick Russell?" I guessed.

"Yup," Delia replied darkly. "I can't believe you saw him selling butterfly orchids at the flea market today."

"What *I* can't believe is that he gets away with those cheesy excuses about getting the orchids from some cousin," Bess added. She took a step back— then yelped in pain as her arm hit the huge cactus behind us.

"Careful! That tree cactus is the rarest thing here," Delia cautioned. "It's the only one in all of the Keys."

"The *only* one?" I echoed, taking a fresh look. No wonder Amira and Dylan had been making such a big deal of it.

As I was about to turn away, I caught sight of something blue lodged in the sharp spikes. "Hmm. Check it out," I said, reaching carefully to get it. "It's a scrap of fabric. Looks like it ripped from a T-shirt."

"It's blue, too, just like the T-shirt the guy in the red boat had on yesterday," Delia said. She stared at the fabric for a moment, then turned to Bess and me. "Did you guys see a blue T-shirt when you were at Chick's houseboat?" she asked. "Maybe one with a hole ripped in it?"

I saw the hope in her eyes, but I had to tell her the truth. "No. Not that I could spot from the window, anyway," I said.

Bess shot a sideways glance at me, and I knew what she was thinking. "What about Steve?" she whispered to me, as we hiked back out of the hardwood hammock a little later. "Did Delia forget that he was wearing a blue T-shirt?"

Actually, I was pretty sure Delia hadn't forgotten. Even though she didn't say anything about it, she was serious and quiet during the hike back to Route 1.

"We've got time for one more stop," she said, as we all got back into her car. "This one's on the bay-side, near the water. We should see butterfly orchids there. And half a dozen other protected species you two might be interested in," she added, nodding at Amira and Dylan.

I figured Delia didn't want to say anything more about the poaching with Dylan and Amira there, so Bess and I kept our thoughts to ourselves. We drove to a different spot and hiked through more jungle. This time we kept going until we saw sawgrass and blue water through the trees, just beyond the hardwood hammock where we stopped.

"Look!" Bess exclaimed. She stopped next to a tree that looked like some kind of oak, covered with dozens of butterfly orchids, which made splashes of bright yellow and brown among the branches. The sight of all those orchids was so gorgeous that we all stopped in our tracks to stare at them.

"Phew! They're all right," Delia said.

A wave of relief washed over me, too. At least the poacher hadn't gotten these. While Dylan and Amira walked around the hammock, pointing at things and making notes, Bess and I sat on a fallen tree trunk and looked out over the water. Now that I wasn't worried about more orchids being taken—at least for the moment—I could appreciate the view. Wind rippled

64

across the blue-green water of the Florida Bay. In the far distance a strip of green marked the mainland. Closer in, I spotted plenty of sails, motorboats, and a few islands.

"Those islands are part of the backcountry," Delia said, stepping over to Bess and me. "You can only get to them by boat. There are dozens of them, actually. Most of them don't have anyone living on them, so they're totally–"

"Hey! Isn't that Steve?" Bess broke in.

A motorboat cruised along the bay just beyond the sawgrass near our hammock. The first thing I noticed was how sleek and new and shiny red it was. Then I saw the face and short blond hair of the boat's one passenger.

"It *is* him!" I said.

This was definitely a surprise, but the true shock came when I noticed what was along one side of the boat: a nasty-looking brown scrape.

8

Backcountry Blues

Steve!" Delia called out. She ran toward the bay, waving, until her sneakers sank into the marshy ground. *"Steve!"*

He must not have been able to hear us over the sound of his motor. Turning the boat away from us, he headed across the bay toward the backcountry.

I was afraid to say what I knew we were all thinking. But someone had to, so I took a deep breath and came out with it.

"Did you see the scrape on his boat? Steve must be the person we chased yesterday," I said.

"I'm really sorry, Delia," Bess added.

Delia just stood there with water up to her ankles, looking dazed. After a moment she turned from the bay and made her way back to the fallen tree trunk where Bess and I sat.

"It couldn't have been him," she told us. "I *know* Steve. He wouldn't steal orchids. If he were here I'm sure he could explain what's going on."

I knew Delia *wanted* to believe that. Still, I could tell by the troubled expression on her face that she knew the evidence was against Steve.

"Um . . . is everything okay?" Dylan called from deeper in the hammock. He and Amira stood with their clipboards next to a funny-looking tree with dull green bark and clusters of leathery leaves.

"Yeah. Fine," Delia said. She went over to the botanists, a shaky smile on her face. "I see you've found the wild dilly, but there are a few other species I wanted to show you."

She shot me a warning glance, and I got the message. Delia obviously didn't want to talk about Steve in front of Dylan and Amira. She looked totally distracted as she led them around, showing them this and that. I felt preoccupied myself, and it wasn't just because we'd seen Steve in that boat. Something nagged at me, like the buzzing, biting cloud of mosquitoes that had followed us all afternoon. But I didn't have a chance to talk to Bess and Delia about it until after Dylan and Amira started on their way back to Tallahassee.

"Okay, here's what I don't get," I said, as soon as their Jeep pulled out of the Pennekamp parking lot. "If Steve was the guy we saw yesterday . . ."

"He wasn't," Delia said firmly. Instead of heading back to her office in the Visitor Center, she walked toward the small beach next to the parking lot. An empty picnic table stood in the shade of some trees, and Delia sat down at it. "At least I hope it wasn't him. Steve doesn't even have a boat."

"Then he must have borrowed that one," Bess said, as we plunked down opposite Delia. "And if he borrowed it today, he could have done the same thing yesterday."

"But what I don't understand," I said, getting back to my point, "is how Chick Russell fits in. He was the one selling butterfly orchids at the flea market. And the way he acted . . . I could have sworn he was up to something weird."

"So it must have been *him* we saw in the red boat yesterday," Delia insisted. I guess she saw the doubt on my face, because she threw up her hands and said, "Come on! What reason could Steve possibly have for stealing protected orchids?"

I almost wished I didn't have an answer for her, but unfortunately I did. "Remember how Mrs. Manning was drooling over the butterfly orchids in the greenhouse yesterday?"

"And today at the flea market, too," Bess added, nodding. "She definitely wanted one."

I could see that Delia got the drift of what we were saying. "You think she convinced *Steve* to steal some for her?" she said, and immediately shook her head. "I really doubt it. I've seen Mrs. Manning's boat. It's white, not red. And if Steve stole orchids for her, then why was she trying to buy a butterfly orchid from Chick at the flea market?"

My head was starting to ache from all the unanswered questions swirling inside it. "Maybe we'd better go right to the source and find out," I suggested.

"You mean, talk to Mrs. Manning? Sure! She'll be able to clear this up." Delia's face brightened, and she jumped up from the picnic table. "Let's see if we can find her at the greenhouse. She paints there most afternoons."

"Mrs. Manning?" Delia said as we stepped through the glass doors and into the steamy greenhouse. "Hello?"

I looked past lush vines and shrubs and trees to the spot where her easel had been set up the day before. Orchids of every size and color were still there, but not the easel.

"That's funny. She's almost always here this time of day," Delia said, frowning.

"Why would she change her routine?" Bess wondered, but Delia just shrugged.

"Who knows? Maybe we can catch up to her

at her house. She lives up at the Ocean Reef Club. That's a gated community north of here, at the very tip of Key Largo."

Leaving our rental convertible at Pennekamp, we drove to the Ocean Reef Club in Delia's car. We had to stop at a security gate at the entrance, and after that we found ourselves in a perfectly manicured world of golf fairways, tennis courts, swimming pools, stucco houses, emerald green lawns, and streets lined with hibiscus, fuchsia, oleander, and royal palms.

"So this is where the country club set hangs out, eh?" Bess said, as a golf cart angled across the road ahead of us. "George would love this place!"

I knew George would love all the sports facilities, but the Ocean Reef Club was almost *too* perfect for me. "I bet there isn't a weed or cracked sidewalk in this whole place," I murmured.

"Probably not," Delia agreed. "Most of the people here are pretty well off—including Mrs. Manning. Steve's dad died a few years back, but I'm pretty sure he was some kind of big corporate executive."

She turned onto a dead-end street with large houses built next to the bay. Mrs. Manning's was the last one, a peach-colored stucco house with lime trees and flowering hibiscus out front. As soon as we parked in the driveway, I heard Mrs. Manning's voice call from the back of the house.

"Back here, Delia! You know the way."

"How'd she know it was us?" Bess said under her breath.

"The security guard," Delia replied. "He has to call before he can let any visitors through the gate."

She led the way along a stone path to the back of the house, where a garden sloped down to a dock at the water's edge. The view was fantastic, with the Card Sound Bridge sloping up and over the bay to the mainland. I spotted an easel standing by itself among some flowering shrubs, but I didn't see Mrs. Manning. At least not until I heard her voice, coming from near the house.

"Those are lovely, Mr. Laughlin," she said. "And we can add more once they get used to their new home here."

I turned and saw a small, glassed-in greenhouse that angled out from the back of the house. Mrs. Manning stood in the doorway talking to an older man wearing a gardener's apron and gloves. When I saw what he was holding, my mouth dropped open.

"You're growing *orchids*?" I asked. All the questions I had expected to ask flew out of my mind. All I could do was stare at the two pots containing bright purple orchids that the gardener held.

"What!" Delia jogged over to the greenhouse, with Bess and me behind her. That was when we saw four *more* orchids—in shades of pink, yellow, and white—on a shelf behind Mr. Laughlin.

"Well, they're not butterfly orchids," Delia murmured, eyeing the blooms. "But . . . didn't you say you gave up on orchids when your last ones died, Mrs. Manning?"

Steve's mother tore her gaze reluctantly away from the orchids. "Well, after seeing those exquisite butterfly orchids you had yesterday, I realized I couldn't just give up on orchids altogether," she told us. "They are so marvelous, and Mr. Laughlin here has the greenest thumb in all of south Florida."

"So you're happy with these?" Bess asked, nodding at the orchids. "Even though they're not as rare and unusual as butterfly orchids?"

I thought I saw a kind of longing in Mrs. Manning's eyes. Then she sighed and said, "I'll admit that I was tempted, darling. But . . . well, if the orchids at the flea market *were* poached, I couldn't encourage that kind of behavior by buying one, could I? And the ones Mr. Laughlin found for me are quite beautiful. I think they'll do marvelously for my paintings."

Delia turned to Bess and me with a triumphant smile. I had to admit that Steve's mother sounded sincere. But now, all the questions I had thought of before came popping back into my head.

"Delia tells us you have a boat, Mrs. Manning," I

said. Stepping away from the greenhouse, I looked toward the dock. Sure enough, a motorboat was tied up there. It was white, just as Delia had said it would be. "Is that it?" I asked, pointing at it.

"Hmm? Oh, yes, that's mine," Mrs. Manning answered. "One of them, anyway."

Delia's smile froze on her face. "One of them?" she repeated.

Mrs. Manning nodded. "I don't suppose you've seen my new boat yet, Delia. It's quite lovely—larger and more powerful, naturally. I think it makes sense to trade up every few years, don't you?"

"Naturally," Bess said, trying not to smile. "As long as you have an extra twenty or thirty thousand dollars lying around," she added under her breath.

"Um, what color is the new one? White, like the one you have already?" Delia asked.

"Actually, I decided to go with something a bit more daring this time," Mrs. Manning told us. "Bright red. It's absolutely irresistible. So much so that Steve has been out on it constantly these past few days. I just hope he takes better care of it today than he did yesterday."

She didn't seem to notice the dire glances that ricocheted among Bess, Delia, and me.

"Why? Did something happen to the boat?" I asked.

"Oh, yes. A large scrape Steve got when he came too close to one of the channel markers," Mrs. Manning said. She frowned thoughtfully. "Ordinarily he's a careful boater, but I suppose accidents do happen."

Especially when you're being chased through the mangrove channels at top speed, I thought. "Um, do you know where Steve is now?" I asked.

"Now that he's quit working with Lucy and Diego Salazar, he could be anywhere," she said. She turned around toward Delia. "You know Steve. He's probably scuba diving or snorkeling along the reef."

"He quit?" Delia said, biting her lip. "He told us he was just taking a few days off."

Mrs. Manning gave a vague wave of her hand. "All I know is that when he came for the boat this morning, he told me the arrangement was permanent."

Bess shot a quick glance at me before asking, "Does Steve ever go diving on the bayside of Key Largo?"

"The bayside?" Steve's mother looked at Bess as if she'd completely lost her mind. "Oh, I doubt it. Without the reef, what would be the point?"

It definitely wasn't the explanation Delia was hoping for.

"I've got to talk to Steve," she told Bess and me, after we said good-bye to Mrs. Manning. "That's the only way we'll really find out what's going on." She pulled her cell phone and car keys from her bag and handed the keys to me. "Nancy, will you drive?"

She must have tried calling him twenty times during the drive back to the Pennekamp parking lot, where Bess and I had left our rental car. He never picked up.

"He's busy, that's all. He'll call back when he can," Delia said.

Judging by the doubtful look on Bess's face, she was just as skeptical as I was. But all she said was, "I hope so."

By the time we got to Delia's, following her in our convertible, the sun was slipping behind the palm trees to the west. It wasn't until I saw the *Island Scout* moored at her dock in the marina—and George sitting on Delia's second-floor balcony—that I remembered where George had been all day.

"Hey! You guys!" she shouted, as soon as she saw us. She practically flew down the stairs to the driveway. "Where've you been? You'll never guess what happened."

George was talking a mile a minute. Her cheeks were flushed and her dark eyes shone with excitement.

"What?" Bess and I asked.

"You're not going to believe this," George told us. "I think we found the *Catarina!*"

9

Treasure-Hunting Tales

Bess, Delia, and I stumbled from our cars, all talk-ing at once. "What!" "You're kidding!" "Where?" "What'd you find?"

"Shhh! I guess I shouldn't be talking so loud," George cautioned, lowering her voice. "I don't think Lucy and Diego want everyone on Key Largo to know about it. But it's *so* cool!"

That was for sure. I was dying for more details, but George was already shooting back up the stairs to Delia's balcony. The rest of us scrambled after her.

As soon as we were inside in the living area, Bess dropped onto the couch. "Is this private enough? Or should we check for listening devices?" she joked, feeling under the cushions.

George was so worked up that she didn't even

have a comeback. "Four gold bars. That's what we found. And a bunch of gold coins—fifty-three, to be precise. Lucy and Diego and I counted them." She sank onto the couch next to Bess and hugged one of the pillows. "Diego says it's worth over fifty thousand dollars. And that's just the beginning. I mean, the rest of the treasure can't be far away, right?"

"Wow! It's like a dream come true," I said, climbing onto one of the stools next to the kitchen counter.

"I *knew* all their hard work would pay off," Delia added. "I can't wait to tell St—"

She stopped in the middle of saying Steve's name. All of a sudden she looked a lot less excited.

"Steve?" George said, finishing Delia's thought. She was so psyched about the *Catarina*'s treasure that she didn't notice Delia's discomfort. "Can you believe he said he didn't think we'd ever find the treasure? He's totally going to eat his words."

Delia's cheeks turned an uncomfortable red. Turning away from George, she stood at the kitchen counter and flipped through the mail she'd grabbed from her mailbox on the way up from the driveway.

"What?" George shot a confused glance at Delia. "Did I say something wrong?" she asked.

"Um, something happened while you were out on the *Scout*," I began. "We saw Steve."

"In a red motorboat . . . with a scrape on it," Bess added.

George blinked, and I could see some of her excitement fade. "Uh-oh," she said.

Delia kept her eyes on the mail while Bess and I told George about seeing Steve—and about our visit with Mrs. Manning.

"So it was the same boat as yesterday, huh?" George said when we were done. "Do you think Steve was . . ."

"Poaching? No way," Delia said firmly, looking over the kitchen counter at us. "Once Steve gets back, he'll be able to explain."

I had a feeling she was waiting for us to agree, but I just couldn't. If Steve had such a great explanation, why was he avoiding Delia's calls?

"Oh, never mind. I'm going to change," Delia said. With that, she headed down the hall to her room. The sound of her bedroom door shutting echoed in the living room until George finally broke the silence.

"She must feel awful," she said, keeping her voice low. "I mean, if Steve was driving that boat, he must be the guy who took those butterfly orchids, right?"

"It's a strong possibility," I agreed.

"His mother definitely has orchids on the brain," Bess pointed out. "She had some gardener working overtime, planting a bunch of new ones in her green-house. There weren't any butterfly orchids, but . . ."

"But maybe that's just because Steve lost the ones he poached when they fell over the back of the boat yesterday?" George guessed.

"Maybe," I agreed. The theory made total sense, but there was a nagging doubt that stuck like glue to the back of my mind. "I just wish I knew where Chick Russell got the butterfly orchids he was selling at the flea market today. Do you think he and Steve know each other?"

"Wait a minute. Back up," George said, glancing from Bess to me. "Chick was selling butterfly orchids? What *else* did I miss?"

We told her everything—from our trip to the flea market, the Shell Emporium, and Chick's houseboat, to finding the scrap of T-shirt fabric near the tree that had been stripped of butterfly orchids.

"So we don't know where Chick got his butterfly orchids," Bess finished. "But that blue fabric could definitely have come from Steve's shirt. Remember he was wearing one when—"

She looked up in surprise as Delia came back into the living room. She had changed into capris and a bright pink scoop-necked T-shirt. It seemed as if she was trying to brighten her mood, too, because she smiled at us and said, "Can we please stop talking about Steve? It's all just guesswork until we talk to him in person. Anyway, I'd much rather hear about the *Catarina*."

George glanced uncertainly at me. She and Bess know how hard it is for me to let go of a mystery once I get started. But I could see that Delia needed cheering up.

"Sounds good to me," I agreed. Turning to George, I said, "What was it like to find those gold bars? Did they look different after sitting at the bottom of the sea for almost four hundred years?"

"I still can't believe you found them at all," Delia added, sinking into a chair by the couch. "Where were they?"

George hesitated. "Lucy and Diego made me promise not to say where we found them," she began.

"Even to us?" Bess said indignantly. "But I'm your cousin! What about blood being thicker than water and all that?"

"It's just till they're sure they've found the mother lode," George said quickly. "Then they'll be able to put out a marker to show they've found a hot spot. You know, treasure from one of the old wrecks."

"Treasure hunters use two red buoys to mark a hot spot," Delia explained to Bess and me. "Other salvage boats will honor the marker and keep at least three hundred feet away so that whoever found the sunken cargo can work the site without other people crowding in."

"The Salazars let me dive, too," George said excitedly. "It was so cool. I mean, at first the gold just looked like old rocks covered with seaweed and barnacles and stuff. But then Diego and Lucy used this blower. . . ." She shook her head in amazement. "Once the sand came off, you could see that it was gleaming."

Listening to George seemed to help Delia take her mind off Steve. To be honest, Bess and I were totally caught up in hearing about the gold too. I had to keep pinching my arm to remind myself that George was talking about real treasure.

"So the Salazars didn't put out the marker?" Delia asked.

"Nope," George said, shaking her head. "They want to make sure they're close enough. Otherwise, some other salvagers could move in and find everything first. Lucy and Diego want to wait and see what happens tomorrow."

"Imagine seeing those gold bars just sitting there at the bottom of the sea," Bess said dreamily. Then she sat up suddenly and said, "Hey! Are they on the *Island Scout* now? Can we see them?"

"Sorry," George said, shaking her head. "The Salazars left, and I'm pretty sure they took the gold with them. At least, they said they were going to keep it safe."

Getting up from the couch, she walked over to the glass doors that led to Delia's balcony. The sun had already sunk below the horizon, and darkness was falling over the marina. "Tomorrow's going to be the big day. I can feel it," George said, gazing at the *Island Scout*. "Diego ran a new scatter pattern on the computer, based on where we found those gold coins and bars today. They said I could go with them again and—"

"Hold on," Bess cut in. "You're going out on the *Scout* again?"

George shot a surprised glance over her shoulder. "Haven't you been listening? They're about to find a huge treasure. Worth millions, maybe! How could I *not* go again? You guys should come too. Diego and Lucy said you could."

"What about the stolen orchids?" Bess wanted to know. Getting up from the couch, she joined George next to the sliding glass doors. "We've got to talk to Steve, and find out more about Chick Russell."

Talk about a touchy situation. Bess looked totally convinced that she was right—and George looked just as sure that *she* was right. The two of them just stood there facing off while Delia and I watched uneasily.

Finally Bess pulled George out onto the balcony. "We'll be right back," she said over her shoulder to Delia and me.

I couldn't hear their conversation, but I had a pretty good idea of what they were saying. Until George suddenly whirled around and said, "Nancy . . . Delia! Come quick!"

There was an urgency in her voice that got me moving fast, and Delia was only half a step behind me.

"Check it out." George pointed to where the *Island Scout* was docked. At first all I saw was the black silhouette of the boat against the dark gray evening sky. Then I spotted it—the glowing yellow flicker of a flashlight beam inside the boat's cabin.

"Someone's sneaking around inside the *Scout!*" I said.

10

Break-in!

We've got to do something!" George gasped. "I mean, what if the Salazars didn't take the gold when they left? What if it's still on board?"

I was already heading for the balcony stairs. Behind me, I heard Delia say, "Shouldn't we call the police? Whoever's there could be dangerous!"

She was right about that, no doubt about it. But there was no way I could stop my feet from running toward the *Scout*. I guess you could say I'm physically incapable of standing still when I come across trouble. I'm hardwired to *do* something about it. And that flickering flashlight beam definitely looked like trouble to me.

"I'll be careful," I called back over my shoulder. That was when I noticed George behind me, her sneakers crunching on the gravel as she ran. Bess and Delia were still on the balcony. From the quick glimpse I got, it looked like Delia was talking into her cell phone.

"Hear that?" George muttered, as we got closer to the *Scout*.

I heard it, all right. Whoever was inside wasn't trying very hard to be quiet. There was a lot of banging and crashing, and the flashlight beam jerked around wildly.

"The Salazars' equipment . . ." I said under my breath.

"That idiot could be destroying it!" George picked up her pace and shot past me, pounding across the dock.

The person inside the boat must have heard her, because the flashlight beam suddenly shined out one of the cabin windows—straight at us.

"Hey!" George paused, blinking into the glare.

Then the light blinked off, and we heard a mad scrambling inside the cabin.

"Quick—before he gets away!" I cried.

We were on the deck in a flash. The cabin door was ajar, and George and I flung it wide and ran inside.

"*Ow!*" George cried, stumbling forward. She hit the cabin floor amid a chaotic mess of metal detectors and oxygen tanks and papers. I saw a flicker of movement in the shadowy darkness beyond George, and then the door on the other side of the cabin banged shut.

"Hey!" I cried, jolting forward. I barely made it past George when I heard a loud splash outside the closed door.

"He's swimming away!" George grimaced, rubbing her shin. She must have seen me hesitate, because she said, "Don't worry about me, Nan. I'm fine. Just go after him!"

It took me only a couple of seconds to yank open the door and get outside. But when I leaned over the railing, all I saw was gently rippling water where the person had jumped in.

Come on, where are you? I wondered.

I scoured the nearby water for any sign of movement, but the marina was a patchwork of boats and docks and buoys, all shrouded in shadows that blocked my view. To make things worse, the steady murmur of voices on the patio of Gaby's Seafood Grille mixed with the sounds of gulls and water lapping against the dock. If someone was swimming, the sounds of it were lost among all the other noises.

"Do you see him?" George asked, limping up next to me. "He can't have gotten far, or—"

Vroom!

The sound of a gunning engine pierced the darkness, making us jump. The next thing we heard was the squeal of tires coming from somewhere near Delia's house. We ran to the front of the boat in time to see a truck zoom past Delia's house before it made a screeching turn and disappeared around a corner. Standing there, listening to the fading sound of the engine, I felt like a deflated balloon.

"I guess we better check on the damage," I said.

Bess and Delia found us inside the *Scout* a minute later. "Whoa," Bess said, looking around with horrified eyes. "Whoever that was really tore this place apart. Do you think he was looking for the gold?"

"Seems like a good guess," I said. George and I had already started to gather up the metal detectors, tools, buoys, and scuba equipment. Talk about total chaos. Every shelf and cabinet had had its contents ripped out and thrown to the floor. Maybe that was why I didn't notice the computer screen right away. But George sure did.

"Uh-oh. Whoever that was tried to log on to the Salazars' computer!" she said.

When I looked over, I saw the message "Access Denied" on the Salazars' computer screen in glowing red letters.

"So he wanted more than just the gold," I realized. "Isn't that the computer Lucy and Diego use to try to predict where the *Catarina* is?"

George nodded. She was already at the keyboard, typing in commands. "Looks like we got here before he could hack into the system and find out where we were today," she said. She lifted her eyes just long enough to glance at Delia and Bess. "Did you two see who was driving that truck? I'm pretty sure he's the one who did this."

"The beat-up one that just tore out of here?" Bess glanced at Delia and shrugged. "There were patches of silver paint on it, but I didn't see who was driving. Sorry."

"Silver paint?" I echoed. That definitely rang a bell, and when I thought about it, I remembered why. "I think I saw that truck yesterday at Pennekamp. It belongs to—"

"Chick Russell!" Delia said, before I could finish. "I can't believe I didn't think of it before. I guess I was too busy calling the police and Lucy and Diego."

"Did you find out about the old coins and gold bars we found? Are they okay?" George asked.

"Diego said not to worry. It's all safe, and he and Lucy are taking extra care to make sure it stays that way," Delia assured her. "Actually, they should be here by the time the police arrive."

Before we knew it, the Salazars and two police officers were crowding into the cabin of the *Island Scout* with us. Once we told them everything that had happened, the officers told us we were free to go. I had a feeling that meant they wanted us out of there so they could look the boat over for evidence—no easy job with four extra people hanging around.

"You usually hate being left out of the loop, Nancy," Bess said, as we made our way back across the marina toward Delia's. She arched an eyebrow at me. "No objections? No sticking around to see what clues the cops dig up? Are you feeling all right?"

"Actually, I was hoping to dig up a few clues of our own," I told her. "Anyone up for a drive to Chick Russell's houseboat?"

The Pelican Bay Trailer Park was a lot livelier at night than when Bess and I had been there before. People were hanging out near their trailers, talking, playing cards, and listening to music, while kids rode bikes and clustered in groups playing electronic games. A few heads turned curiously our way as we drove toward the houseboats along a road sparsely lit by streetlamps.

"Hmm," Bess said, as I pulled our convertible into the empty spot next to Chick's houseboat. The inside of the boat was completely dark. We looked up and down the row of parking spaces that ran alongside the docks, but Chick's truck wasn't there.

"What do we do now?" Delia asked, frowning.

George nodded at a middle-aged couple who sat on the rear deck of the boat right next to Chick's. Both of them were staring right at us.

"We can't sneak on board to take a look around," George whispered. "Not with Mr. and Mrs. Busybody sitting two feet away."

The neighbors kept glancing our way, and finally the man came to the railing and said, "Can we help you folks with something?"

Hmm, I thought. If these people were as nosy as they looked, maybe they *could* help us. Putting on my friendliest smile, I got out of our convertible and walked over to their boat. "Actually, we're looking for Chick Russell," I told them. "Have you seen him?"

"I don't recall seeing you here before," the woman spoke up. She looked over her glasses at me, then peered at Delia, Bess, and George in the car. "Are you friends of Chick's?"

"More like acquaintances," I said, wishing she'd stop giving us the third degree. "We'd like to, um, interview Chick. You know, for a kind of personal profile of a local businessman."

It wasn't a *total* lie. I mean, we did want to talk to him, even if the information was for solving a crime and not for any newspaper article. Luckily, they didn't question my explanation.

"Is that right? Well, Chick *is* a born salesman, that's

the truth," the man said, chuckling. "You never know what he'll be selling next."

"We saw corals this morning at the flea market," Bess said. She, Delia, and George were all out of the car now, and they walked over to join me. "And orchids. Real beauties."

"You don't happen to know where he gets them, do you?" Delia added.

The woman sat back in her chair and shook her head. "It's a mystery to me where he gets all that stuff," she told us. "Every so often we see him carrying a crate of this or a bucket of that, but Chick doesn't give a lot of particulars."

No surprise there. If Chick was poaching, he wouldn't exactly advertise.

"Anyhow, I guess you'd be better off asking him yourself," the woman's husband added. "Here he is now, as a matter of fact."

A pair of headlights arced out over the bay as Chick's truck pulled up next to our convertible. For a moment he sat behind the wheel, taking in the situation. When he finally got out, I saw Bess, George, and Delia all do double takes. Apparently they'd noticed the same thing I had—that Chick's hair, sneakers, shorts, and shirt were soaking wet.

"Hello, Chick," Delia said, eyeing him from head to toe. "Been out for a swim?"

If he was at all bothered by her scrutiny, he didn't show it. He smiled broadly and said, "Well, this is a surprise. To what do I owe the pleasure of your visit, ladies?" He didn't answer Delia's question, I noticed. But I wasn't going to let him off the hook that easily.

"Someone broke into the *Island Scout* tonight, over at Rock Harbor," I told him.

"Someone who jumped into the water to get away from us," George added. "And then drove off in a truck that looks exactly like yours."

Chick scratched his chin, seeming to consider what they had said. "The *Island Scout*? Is that some kind of boat?" he asked.

I caught the doubtful glances Bess and George shot my way. Could Chick really be so clueless? I didn't think so. I noticed that he totally ignored the fact that we'd seen his truck there. And that his soaking wet clothes made him a suspect.

"Yes, it's a boat," Bess said patiently. "We told the police about seeing your truck there, by the way. And now here you are looking like you've just been for a swim in your clothes. I'm sure the officers on the case will be very interested to hear that."

You can bet the couple on the neighboring houseboat were hanging on our every word. They didn't even try to pretend they weren't eavesdropping.

"What kind of journalists are those girls?" I heard the man whisper to his wife. "I thought they were going to ask about his merchandise."

As Chick glanced at his neighbors, I saw the corners of his mouth lift in a smirk. Then he turned back to us and said, "Far as I know, there's no law says a man can't take a dip in his clothes. Now, if you *journalists* don't mind, I'd like to go inside and take a shower."

I couldn't believe it. Somehow, Chick was twisting everything around to make it look like *we* were the ones with something to hide. Okay, maybe we had been busted misrepresenting our motives to his neighbors. But as far as I was concerned, Chick still had some serious explaining to do. I could tell Delia felt the same way.

"Actually, we do have some questions for you," she said, stepping in front of him. "What were you doing on the—"

"Would you look at the time? Sorry, ladies, but it's getting late," Chick cut in. "Why don't you stop by during business hours, and we'll finish our little chat?"

Chick didn't give us time to object. Grabbing his digital music player from the dashboard, he slammed the truck door, stepped past Delia, hopped onto the dock, and went inside his boat.

That left just us and his nosy neighbors. They were watching us like we were the hottest prime-time reality show on network TV. Too weird. So we got into our car and drove back down the winding drive toward Route 1.

"Does that guy ever give a straight answer?" Bess asked. "I mean, it's obvious he's the one who was on the *Scout*."

"His attitude really bugs me," I admitted. "But we can't let him get to us. We have to be objective if we're going to figure out what Chick is up to."

"Isn't it obvious? He was trying to get the gold coins and gold bars we found today!" George said.

"Yes, but . . ." I took a deep breath, trying to make sense of all the thoughts and questions that kept popping up in my head. "How could Chick know about the gold in the first place? Until now we figured he's probably poaching. Maybe even poaching on a pretty big scale. But stealing sunken treasure? Does Chick even know Lucy and Diego?"

I looked at Delia in the rearview mirror. "Hmm? Oh—not that I know of," she said. But she was staring out the window, as if her mind was on something else. When I checked the mirror again, she was fishing around in her bag, and then I heard her pressing keys on her cell phone. She listened for a while, then hung up and tossed the phone back into her bag.

"Steve?" Bess guessed.

Delia nodded. "Still no answer," she said, letting out a sigh. "I don't get it. Why won't he call me back?"

I wasn't sure what to say. It seemed pretty clear to me that Steve was avoiding Delia. Up until now, she had been his staunchest defender. But now, as she stared out from the backseat, absently drumming her fingers against the door, I thought I saw a glimmer of doubt.

11

Unanswered Questions

I still think you're making a mistake, George," Bess said, as we ate breakfast on Delia's balcony the next morning. "How can you think of going out on the *Island Scout* when we still haven't caught the guy who poached those orchids?"

It was way too early in the morning for me. The sun was barely up over the horizon, but I'd dragged myself out of bed when I'd heard George's alarm. It seemed like we'd gone to bed the night before with so many unanswered questions—about Chick, the break-in of the Salazars' boat, and what Steve was up to. I figured the earlier we got started trying to answer them, the better.

If Bess and George could work out their differences.

"I can't miss being there when they find the *Catarina*. I just can't," George argued. Plunking her empty coffee mug down on the table, she reached into the sports bag that sat at her feet. A second later, she took out a bottle of sunscreen and started rubbing it on her face and arms. "You understand, right, Delia?"

"Hmm?" Delia glanced up from her toast and coffee. "Sure, you should go," she told George. "I don't know what we're going to be able to find out here, anyway."

She sounded glum, and there were circles under her eyes, as if she hadn't slept well. I noticed that Delia's cell phone lay on the table next to her plate. She'd already checked it about twenty times to see if it was working.

It made me feel awful to see her looking so down. She seemed totally different from the smiling, energetic person who'd greeted us when we got to Key Largo. I guess I could understand how she felt. It had to be devastating to think her own boyfriend might be breaking the law, especially when he could be taking plants that she worked really hard to protect. I figured the best way I could help was to do everything possible to learn the truth.

"We can start by finding out what the police learned when they checked out the Salazars' boat last night," I suggested. Getting up from the table, I looked over the balcony railing toward the marina. "Diego and Lucy are already there. Let's go talk to them before they head out."

"Before *we* head out, you mean," George corrected.

Bess rolled her eyes but didn't argue. I guess she realized George wasn't about to change her mind. Within a few minutes, we were all on our way to the *Scout*.

The rising sun gave a hint of the heat that would build later, but this early in the day, the breeze off the water was still refreshing. Low-slanting rays bathed the docks and boats—including the *Scout*—in a golden pink glow.

"You girls are just in time," Diego called out from the deck. He lugged a garbage bag to the railing and handed it down to us. "Lucy and I are about done cleaning up, but we could use a hand getting these bags to the Dumpster."

Lucy was behind him, holding a second bag, which she handed down too. "We're lucky that intruder didn't wreck anything important. Just some papers, manuals, and food," she said. "And a printer that broke when it was knocked to the floor."

"Your computer's okay?" George asked. "The software programs and navigational equipment? The digging tools and that blower thing you used yesterday to clear sand from the gold bars?"

"All fine," Diego assured her. "I double-checked the scuba equipment, too. None of the wet suits or oxygen tanks were damaged either." He winked at George and said, "So, are you ready to find some treasure?"

"Definitely!" George didn't waste a second getting on board. She and the Salazars seemed eager to get going, but they held back long enough to tell us that the police hadn't found anything unusual when they'd searched the *Scout*.

"Nothing?" said Bess. "You're sure?"

Lucy shrugged. "The police thought the same thing we did—that someone must have been looking for the old coins and gold bars we found yesterday. They made a mess doing it, but there's no real damage," she said. "The officers told us they'd be talking to that fellow whose truck you saw."

"Chick Russell," Delia said.

"That's the one. We should be hearing from them after they speak to him, but they haven't been in touch yet," Lucy said. "Thank goodness you girls stopped him before he could retrieve information from our computer system."

"Of course, we still haven't figured out how anyone could know about the gold in the first place," Diego added. "We've never even met any Chick Russell that I can remember. And we didn't tell a soul about the gold."

"Neither did we," George promised.

It was the same question that had bothered me the night before: How could Chick know about the gold George and the Salazars had found? It was disappointing to learn that Lucy and Diego didn't have an answer either. "Maybe the police will learn more when they talk to Chick," I said.

"Let's hope so," Diego said. "Ready to help with those ropes, Delia?"

She had barely said a word since we'd gotten to the marina. But as she handed the first mooring line over to Diego, she suddenly blurted out, "Have you heard from Steve? I was hoping . . . well, that he might be here."

Diego shook his head. "We haven't heard from him since yesterday morning, when he called to say he's quitting our operation."

So it was true, I thought. Steve *did* quit.

"I tried calling him to let him know about yesterday's find. I thought he might change his mind," Diego went on. "But he never picked up."

"At least Delia's not the only one getting the silent treatment from Steve," Bess said to me under her breath.

I wasn't sure that made Delia feel any better. She stood on the dock, frowning and squinting into the sun, until the *Island Scout* motored out of Rock

Harbor. Then, all at once, she shook herself and turned to Bess and me.

"Let's do something fun today," she said.

Bess and I looked at each other. "What about the poaching?" Bess asked.

"We can find out more about Chick and . . . and everything else this afternoon," Delia said. "But I'll feel awful if you guys don't see some of the sights while you're here. Besides," she added, with a shaky smile, "I really don't want to hang around here worrying about what Steve might be up to."

When she put it that way, how could we refuse? "Well?" I asked, raising an eyebrow at Bess.

She grinned back at me. "What are we waiting for? I'm dying to see the reef!" she said.

After changing into our bathing suits, we drove to Pennekamp and rented snorkeling equipment and a motorboat. Before we knew it, we were heading out toward the ocean along the same mangrove-lined channel we'd taken our first day in Key Largo. This time, we didn't see any suspicious-looking boats—just pelicans, egrets, and some bird with a yellow-tufted head that sat atop one of the channel markers.

"There are nine diving sites inside the park," Delia explained. "But Molasses Reef is the biggest, and the snorkeling is fantastic. It's a few miles offshore, so it'll take us awhile to get there."

Not that Bess and I minded. The deep–blue water and sky stretched out endlessly in front of us, and whenever we looked back we saw the tree-lined shore and a lighthouse off to the southwest. I couldn't believe it when a pair of dolphins jumped up in a graceful arc right next to us as they raced alongside the boat. The salty sea breeze felt fantastic, and it made the sun seem a little less intense.

"This is the place," Delia said, cutting the engine and reaching for the anchor. She pointed to our right. "Actually, the reef is over there. We'll drop anchor here where there's no coral, and then swim over."

The next hour was unbelievable. Just a few feet beneath the surface was an underwater world of tubes, fans, pillars, horns, whips, ledges, channels and walls—all made of coral. Some were pink, while others were yellow, orange, brown, white, purple, and even an amazing peacock blue. Coral fans and flowers waved gently in the current alongside harder corals that looked like all sorts of things: brains, lettuce, stars, fingers, and even the horns of a deer. Tropical fish swam by in flashes of neon blue, yellow, and orange, darting in and out of the coral caves and nooks and channels.

"I don't know what's more beautiful," Bess said, as we treaded water after exploring for a while. "The reef, or all the fish and things swimming around it!"

"It *is* amazing," Delia agreed. "More than three hundred kinds of tropical fish live here. Not to mention manta rays, sponges, coral shrimp, crabs, and lobsters. That's one reason protecting the reef is so important. Coral grows really slowly, less than an inch a year."

"So when poachers take coral, or the reef gets damaged by boaters who run into it, they could be destroying hundreds of years of growth," I said, doing the math in my head. I knew it was the same story for rare plants like butterfly orchids. They could become extinct, too. As we swam back to the boat and toweled off, I felt all the more determined to do something about it.

"Are you guys ready to head back?" I asked.

Bess was soaking up some rays on the back bench seat, with her eyes closed and her sunglasses on. She nodded vaguely and mumbled, "Wake me up when we get there, okay?"

Delia was sitting on her towel behind the wheel, but I wasn't sure she'd heard me. Then I saw the cell phone she was holding to her ear, and the hurt expression on her face. Obviously, Steve still wasn't answering her calls.

"Maybe it's not such a good idea to keep calling him," I said, glancing toward shore. "If we want to get answers from Steve, we should probably talk to him in person. How far are we from the Ocean Reef Club?"

"You think Steve could be at his mother's?" Delia asked.

Bess lifted her head, squinting at us over the tops of her sunglasses. "Why not?" she asked. "He uses her boat, right? And it was barely light when we saw George off, so it must still be pretty early."

"Nine-thirty," Delia said, checking her watch. "You're right! If we hurry, we might get there before Steve heads out."

She started the engine, her face filled with determination. I knew we were taking a chance. Steve might have left already, or he might not be using his mother's boat today. But I couldn't help thinking that whatever we found out would be better than calling a cell phone number he obviously wasn't answering.

As Delia steered our boat toward the northern end of the island, the solid mangroves along the Coral Reef State Park gave way to the golf greens, marinas, and resort condos of the Ocean Reef Club. After rounding a point where some windsurfers cut across the water past a beach with a volleyball net set up on it, we headed around to the bayside. Delia cruised past smaller channels lined with condominiums and private docks. Before long, the Card Sound Bridge came into view, and I caught sight of Mrs. Manning's peach-colored stucco house.

"Her new boat's there," Delia said, pointing. "And so's Steve!"

It was easy to see the bright red boat, moored opposite the white one at her dock. Steve stood on the dock next to it. As we watched, he stepped on board to put something in the back of the boat.

"What *is* that?" I wondered, but we were too far away to see clearly.

"Steve!" Delia called out, as we got closer.

Steve straightened up in the back of the boat and turned our way. He peered at us, shading his eyes, then quickly turned away again. In the next instant, we saw him frantically shaking out a blue tarp.

"What's he doing, hiding something?" Bess wondered.

Delia didn't answer, but as we got closer I saw the way her eyes zeroed in on the bulky mound covered by the blue tarp.

"Oh, great. He's already been out," she said, groaning. "And whatever he poached is right under that tarp."

12

Steve's Story

Delia . . . hi!" **Steve called,** in a voice that sounded falsely bright to me. He smiled at us, but there was a wary glint in his eyes. "What are you guys doing here?"

"Looking for you," Delia told him. Her cheeks were an angry red as she maneuvered our boat up to the dock. Cutting the motor, she jumped onto the dock before Bess and I even had time to tie us up to the mooring post. "Apparently, this is the only way to talk to you, since you're not answering your cell phone. Or calling me back."

"Look, Delia . . . ," Steve began. He shot an uneasy glance at the tarp, but that just made Delia angrier.

"I can't believe I've been defending you!" she said, climbing right onto the red boat and jabbing a finger at the tarp. "What are you hiding under there? Corals? More orchids?"

Bess and I finished tying up our boat just as Delia yanked on a corner of the tarp.

"Don't!" Steve yelled. He tried to stop Delia, but it was too late. The tarp flew off, revealing the bulky load underneath.

Bess pushed her sunglasses up on top of her head and glared at Steve. "What's going on?" she asked.

I was wondering the same thing myself. Heaped in the bottom of the boat were all kinds of digging tools: two shovels, a couple of pickaxes, a big metal sledgehammer, and some smaller trowels and rakes. At first, all I could do was stare, trying to make sense of it.

"You wouldn't need all this heavy stuff to poach orchids," I said, thinking out loud. "A little knife would be enough."

"Poach?" Steve held up a hand and shook his head back and forth. "You've got it all wrong. I'm not poaching. I'm—"

He stopped short and clamped his mouth shut.

"What?" Delia insisted, looking him right in the eye. "Why can't you tell me? If you're not breaking the law, then what are you being so secretive about?"

I guess she finally got through to Steve, because he looked pretty embarrassed. "Look, I didn't want to say anything until after I found it, but you're right. I owe you the truth," he began.

"About time," Bess said under her breath.

Steve shoved his hands into the pockets of his shorts and blew out a long breath. "I've been looking for pirate's gold," he said.

"Pirate's gold?" Delia stared at him, as if she wasn't sure she'd heard him right. "You're kidding, right?"

"No. And that's exactly why I didn't say anything before. I knew you wouldn't take me seriously," Steve said. He sat down on the bench seat that ran along the side of the boat. "Look, everyone knows pirates were all over the Keys back in the old days. Jean Lafitte, Gasparilla, John Rackham, Henry Morgan . . . They hid treasure all over the place."

"Really?" Bess's eyes lit up as she gazed out at the bay. "Sunken ships, pirate's gold . . . This place gets more exotic and mysterious every minute," she said.

Key Largo did have a fairy-tale past, but that didn't change the fact that everything we'd learned about the poached orchids pointed to Steve as a very real bad guy.

"Are you trying to tell us that when we chased you in the mangroves, you *weren't* poaching orchids? You were looking for pirate's treasure?" I asked.

Steve shifted uncomfortably on the bench seat. "I didn't poach anything, I promise," he said. "Maybe I'd better start at the beginning. A couple of days ago, it suddenly hit me that the Salazars might never find the *Catarina*. I mean, why would they? No one else has."

"Actually . . . ," Bess began, but Steve didn't give her a chance to finish.

"So I bought a map," he went on. "The real thing—on this old parchment that's practically falling apart. Chick swears it was made by Jean Lafitte himself and—"

"Wait a minute. You got the map from *Chick*?" Delia interrupted. "That guy would cheat his own mother! It's probably a fake, Steve."

"You don't have to be so cynical," he said. "Take a look for yourself if you don't believe me."

You can bet Bess and I weren't going to miss out on *that*. We scrambled onto the red motorboat as Steve opened a storage compartment next to the bench seat. He pulled out a mottled brown parchment that looked so old and weathered it was hard to make out the ink markings on it. The edges were frayed and crumbling, and in some places there were holes in it. I had to look closely to see the crudely drawn map and faded, old-fashioned handwriting.

"Wow," Bess said, tilting her head to the side while she scrutinized the map. "Too bad I can't make heads or tails of this thing."

"It's kind of hard to read," Steve agreed. "That's because Lafitte buried the treasure in the backcountry. Keeping all the islands straight isn't easy. There's Calusa Key, Buttonwood, Manatee, Rabbit Keys . . ."

As I listened, something about his explanation felt wrong to me. I just couldn't put my finger on what it was.

"That one there, with the X, is where the treasure is," Steve went on, pointing. "I was sure it was Black Betsy Key, but when I went there yesterday—"

"I hate to break it to you, Steve," Delia interrupted, "but I don't think this map is as old as it looks."

"Huh?" Steve glanced up, frowning. "What do you mean?"

"Check it out," Delia said. She'd been fingering a corner of the parchment. Now she gently scratched it with her fingernail, scraping away the weathered brown surface and revealing a fresh white layer underneath.

"That doesn't look very old," Bess commented.

Delia nodded. "Exactly. I think Chick must have taken a new parchment and scraped it thin, then burned the edges and stained the surface with tea or something to make it *look* old," she said.

"That can't be right," Steve insisted. But when he scratched at another spot, the same thing happened. "I don't believe this," he muttered. "I spent the last two days buzzing all over the backcountry trying to find the right island, and now I find out my map isn't even real!"

"The backcountry?" I repeated. I blinked as it hit me. "That's it!" I snapped my fingers. "*That's* what didn't feel right to me!"

Delia, Bess, and Steve all stared at me as if I were some kind of alien that had suddenly beamed down from another planet.

"Steve," I said, turning to him, "you told us you were looking for Lafitte's treasure in the backcountry, right?"

"Yeah," he said, shrugging. "So?"

"*So* . . . the mangrove trails where we chased you aren't anywhere near the backcountry," I pointed out. "They're on the total opposite side of Key Largo. You couldn't have been in both places at once."

"You're right!" Delia breathed. Crossing her arms in front of her, she shot a piercing look at her boyfriend. "No more lies, Steve. I want the truth."

Steve glanced nervously down at his feet. "It wasn't me," he mumbled.

He must have realized how lame he sounded, because he quickly went on, "Really. It's the truth! Look, when I bought the map, I didn't exactly pay with money. I traded certain . . . services."

"Huh? What kind of services?" Bess asked, crinkling

up her nose. But I thought I had a pretty good idea of what he was talking about.

"You lent Chick your mother's boat?" I guessed.

Steve nodded and said, "I couldn't believe it when he brought it back with that huge scrape on it. He told me he banged it when he came too close to a channel marker."

"So you gave the same phony story to your mother, right?" Bess said.

"I didn't know it was a lie," Steve insisted. "If I'd known Chick was going to use the boat to poach orchids, I never would have lent it to him."

For the first time since we'd arrived in Key Largo, I found myself believing him. Maybe the guy had made some dumb choices, but it didn't look like he was poaching. "That would explain why the guy in the boat wore a baseball cap like Chick's," I said, thinking out loud. "It *was* Chick."

"Hey!" Delia said, straightening up all of a sudden. "We can't just sit around here. Not when Chick could be out in the park poaching something right now."

I felt a little bad about leaving Steve after dropping the bombshell that his treasure map was a fake, but Delia was right. We needed to find out what Chick was up to—and the sooner the better.

"We'll call you later," Delia said, as we got back on

board the motorboat we'd taken from Pennekamp. We were just pulling away from the dock when she snapped her fingers. "Oh—I almost forgot to tell you," she called back to Steve. "The Salazars are closing in on the *Catarina*. They think they're going to hit the mother lode today!"

"What?" Steve cupped a hand around his ear, yelling over the sound of the motor.

Delia started to tell him again, but then she just waved and said, "Never mind. . . . I'll tell you later!"

"Boy, is he going to be in for a surprise," Bess said, as we motored back around the northern tip of Key Largo.

"I'll say," I agreed.

"Maybe I should feel sorry for him," Delia said, tucking her hair behind her ears. "But I just keep thinking how crazy it was for him to trust Chick in the first place. If he'd just been honest with us . . ."

"We would have found out a lot sooner that it was Chick who we chased in the mangrove trails," I finished.

Bess's long hair blew out behind her as Delia picked up speed. "I guess the lure of treasure can make people do crazy things, huh?" she said.

I had to agree. Even as she said it, I found myself wondering what crazy things Chick might be up to. I must have checked my watch a zillion times during the boat ride back to Pennekamp. It was already late morning, and Chick could be anywhere, taking coral, or orchids, or some other rare thing to sell on the black market. The more impatient I got, the slower time seemed to pass. It took forever before we were back at the marina in Pennekamp.

"Where to now?" Bess wondered, as we hurried to Delia's car.

"Chick's houseboat," I said, without hesitating. "He might not be there, but maybe we'll find some clue to where he is."

It only took about five minutes to drive to the Pelican Bay Trailer Park. As we made our way along the winding road to the bay, I kept an eye out for Chick's truck, but I didn't see it anywhere.

"Doesn't seem like he's around," I said, as we pulled into the empty spot next to his boat.

"Looks like the neighbors might be out too," Delia commented, glancing at the empty chairs on the deck of the boat next to Chick's. "At least we won't get the third degree while we look around."

The three of us got out of Delia's car and quickly made our way to Chick's houseboat. I didn't see any sign of movement inside. Bess kept glancing nervously next door. Maybe she expected the neighbors to suddenly pop out and surprise us.

"Hey—do you guys hear that?" Delia said, as she

stepped onto the rear deck of Chick's boat.

When I stopped to listen, I *did* hear it. "Voices," I said. "I guess Chick is home after all."

I strode over to the door and knocked loudly.

"Hello?" I called. "Chick?"

Inside, the voices kept on without the slightest pause. It sounded like they were right on the other side of the door, but when I pressed my face against the Plexiglas, I didn't see anyone. Except for the clothes and dishes and things that were scattered around, Chick's living area and galley looked deserted.

"Weird," I said.

"Hey, wait a minute!" Bess said, coming up behind me. "I know those voices. . . ."

As soon as she said it, I realized that I recognized them too. "It's George!" I said. "And Lucy and Diego Salazar!"

13

Race to the *Catarina*

"**H**ow is that possible?" Delia asked, gaping at Bess and me. "They're out on the *Island Scout!*"

"I don't know, but we'd better find out," I said, peering into the boat again. It *looked* empty, but I still heard George's voice. It sounded like she was asking a question, and then I heard Diego's deeper voice answering.

"Too weird. Where *are* they?" I murmured.

I glanced furtively around, but I didn't see anyone watching us. "Here goes," I said. I turned the doorknob and pushed—and the door opened.

"Excellent!" Bess said approvingly from behind me. She practically pushed me over in her hurry to get inside. "George?" she called softly.

The voices were clearer now. They seemed to be

coming from the table in the living area.

"It's coming from the stereo!" I realized.

Sure enough, George's voice was coming from the speakers. "Here's another one, Lucy," she was saying.

"Great," I heard Lucy say. "Thanks, George, I've got it."

I heard splashing, and then the *thunk* of something heavy being put down. "Oh my gosh!" I said. "We can hear everything that's happening on board the *Scout* right now!"

"Huh?" Delia murmured. But I wasn't sure she'd heard me. She and Bess were sitting on Chick's couch, so focused on the voices that they didn't even glance my way.

I ran my finger along the plastic-coated wire that was plugged into the speakers. The other end of the wire was connected to a silver, palm-sized, digital music player. I suddenly knew exactly where I'd seen it before. Chick had been wearing it when Bess and I saw him at the Key Largo flea market.

"Except it's not really an audio player at all," I said out loud. "It's a listening device!"

"Come again?" Bess shook herself and turned to stare at me. "What are you talking about, Nancy?"

"Chick has been eavesdropping," I said. "He must have put some kind of bug on the *Island Scout*.

Remember when we were at the flea market and he had those earphones on?"

"That's right!" said Bess. "I thought it was just music, but he must have been listening to George and the Salazars!"

Delia nodded, and her eyes widened. "He had the earphones last night, too. He took them from his truck right before he went inside, remember?"

"Which means he's been eavesdropping on the *Island Scout* for at least two days," I said. "Well, that explains how he knew about the coins and gold bars George and Lucy and Diego found yesterday. But"—I glanced curiously around the small houseboat—"where is he *now*? Why'd he *stop* listening to what's going on aboard the *Scout*?"

Delia and Bess looked worriedly at each other. The sounds and voices on the boat had been a steady murmur in the background while we talked. Now we heard Diego say, "There must be four or five *hundred* gold bars down there, Lucy. And look what George and I just found!"

Again I heard splashing, and the heavy sounds of something hitting the deck.

"My goodness . . . look at that old box! Is it cedar?" came Lucy's fascinated voice.

"That's what Diego thinks," George told her. "It's full of jewelry. Gold, emeralds, rubies . . ."

The incredible excitement in their voices came through loud and clear, even over the speakers. Bess, Delia, and I were all totally speechless. But finally Bess found her voice.

"They got it!" she squealed. "They found the mother lode from the *Catarina!*"

"Gold bars, gems . . . ," Delia marveled. "It sounds more magnificent than I ever imagined." All of a sudden she jolted upright, gasping. "Oh my gosh . . . *that's* why Chick's not here. He knows they found the *Catarina's* treasure too!"

As soon as the words were out of her mouth, I knew she was right. "Of course! He knows . . . and he's going to steal it. Chick must have heard George and the Salazars say where they are, and now he's going after them!"

I went into the sleeping quarters at the back of Chick's boat. As soon as I looked out the small windows there, my suspicion was confirmed. "His boat's gone," I announced.

"Which means that George and Diego and Lucy could be in danger," Bess called back.

I was about to rejoin her and Delia when I caught sight of something blue on the floor next to the bed. "Hey," I murmured, "a T-shirt."

Sure enough, when I picked it up, I saw that a piece had ripped from the sleeve. "Check it out," I said as I went back into the living area. I held out the shirt, wiggling a finger through the hole in the sleeve.

Delia took one look and grinned at me. "Mr. Rinaldi will be glad to see that. If it matches the scrap we found, it proves that Chick is the one who stripped all those butterfly orchids from the tree we saw," she said.

"But what should we do now?" Bess asked. "A guy who poaches endangered species and breaks into other people's boats isn't exactly going to respect a marker telling people to stay three hundred feet away. How are we going to warn George and the Salazars?"

Good question. I pictured George and the Salazars, totally oblivious to the fact that Chick knew exactly where they were and was probably on his way there. On the speakers, we heard the three of them still exclaiming over the box of jewels.

"Well, at least Chick's not there yet—we'd hear him if he was." I took my cell phone from my bag and punched in George's number, but the call was routed to her voice mail. After leaving a message for her to call, I hung up.

"What about Diego and Lucy? Can you contact them?" I asked Delia, but she shook her head.

"They always turn their phones off when they

dive," she told us. "They might not check for messages until after they're back in the Rock Harbor marina."

"Which means that George and the Salazars are on their own," Bess finished.

Delia sank her chin into her hands, frowning. "I can't believe Steve actually did favors for Chick," she said. "Chick is trying to cheat our friends . . . to steal treasure he doesn't have any right to. And Steve actually *helped* him."

No doubt about it, Steve wasn't going to win any Most Faithful Friend awards. I even wondered if maybe *he'd* been the one who put the listening device on the *Island Scout* in the first place, as one of his "favors" to Chick.

"We can't change what happened. All we can do is figure out what to do next," I said.

A pad and pencil lay on the table next to the speakers. As I listened to George and Diego and Lucy talking, I picked up the pencil, ready to write down anything that might help us find them.

"Hey," I murmured, staring at the pad. "Maybe there's another way. . . ."

I picked up the pad and tilted it in the light. "We could try taking a rubbing of whatever Chick wrote down on this pad," I suggested. "See those indentations? It looks like he pressed down so hard that the pencil made marks on the page underneath."

Gently, I rubbed the pencil across the blank page. When I was done, we all leaned over to get a look at the indented marks that were left in white:

25*19N

80*38W

"Is that some kind of code?" Bess wondered.

"They're map coordinates!" Delia said. "Latitude and longitude. At least, I'm pretty sure that's what they are. If we look at a map, I bet we'll find that they mark a spot somewhere along the reef."

That was all I needed to hear. Ripping the paper from the pad, I jumped to my feet. "We don't know how much of a head start Chick has. Let's go!"

Luckily, the Pelican Bay Trailer Park was close to Pennekamp. Within twenty minutes we were back in one of the state park motorboats. As Delia steered down the mangrove channel from the marina, I barely noticed the tropical birds perched among the branches and on the channel markers. I guess I was too focused on looking for Chick's boat to appreciate the tropical scenery. Tons of kayaks and motorboats were out on the water, but I didn't catch sight of any weathered, blue-green hull that might be Chick's.

Delia had gotten binoculars and a nautical chart from her office, and she consulted the chart as we cleared the mangroves and headed for the open water. "The coordinates Chick wrote down mark a spot that's down from Molasses Reef and a little farther out," she told Bess and me. "When we get close, we can keep an eye out for the *Scout*."

I knew we wouldn't be within sight of the *Scout* for twenty minutes or so, but I kept gazing ahead anyway. The afternoon sun sparkled blindingly on the water, so we had to use the binoculars to get a clear look at boats in the distance. We must have passed half a dozen fishing boats, some sailboats, and a tour boat from Pennekamp. Just when I thought that maybe we'd gotten the coordinates wrong, Bess pointed ahead and said, "What about that one? Isn't that the *Scout*?"

I peered into the distance. Out past a fishing boat was another boat that looked about the right shape to be the *Island Scout*. It was too far away to see clearly, but Bess was looking through the binoculars.

"Yes! I see George on the deck and . . . wow! Look at all those gold bars," she said. "It looks like there's a mountain of them!"

"What about Chick?" I asked.

"Oh—right." Bess moved the binoculars left and right. "Looks like we got here first. I don't see

Chick or his boat anywhere," she reported.

That was definitely good news. I wasn't sure how we'd managed it. But figuring that out wasn't nearly as important as making sure George, Diego, and Lucy were safe.

By the time we passed the fishing boat, I could see the *Scout* more clearly—and the two red buoys that floated right next to her. George was by herself on the deck, wearing a wet suit. As Delia steered around the buoys, Bess and I waved and shouted, "George!"

It took her about half a second to realize who we were. "Great! You decided to come after all! Boy, did you ever make the right decision. Check it out!" she cried, grabbing our mooring line from Bess. "Can you believe how much gold we found? We're still not done bringing it all up. Diego and Lucy are getting another load from the bottom now."

George was even more excited than she'd been the day before. And as we climbed onto the *Scout*, I saw why. I had never seen so much gold. A wall of it, five bars wide and the whole length of the deck, stood gleaming in the sun. Next to the bars were buckets of gold coins, chains, knobs of silver that looked like candlesticks, and silverware.

"You're not going to believe what's in here," George said. Beaming, she bent to touch an ancient-looking wooden box with a carved top. "It's—"

"Jewelry. Gold, rubies, emeralds — we know all about it, George," Bess said.

"Huh?" George shot a cockeyed glance at her cousin, then laughed. "Yeah . . . right."

"It's the truth. Chick Russell bugged the *Scout*," Delia explained. "He's been listening to everything you guys have been saying."

Once we started talking, we couldn't stop. The three of us tripped over our words in our hurry to get the story out. George listened with this half-confused look on her face. But all at once, I could tell she got it.

"Wait a minute. Chick Russell is coming here? *Now?* I've got to warn Lucy and Diego!" George strode over to a rope that was looped through a pulley and stretched down below the water. "We've been loading the treasure into a wire basket that's tied to the end of this. Two tugs is the signal to come up," she said, yanking twice on the rope. "The bottom's only about twenty feet down, so they'll be up right away."

We waited, but after a minute, Lucy and Diego still hadn't surfaced.

"What's going on?" George murmured.

We gazed over the railing, but the water wasn't clear enough to see to the bottom. George tugged on the rope again, and this time, two heads popped up above the surface of the water.

"Finally! I was starting to get worried," George said.

Diego and Lucy pulled off the mouthpieces from their oxygen tanks. I would have expected them to look excited, but the faces behind their goggles were grim.

"What's the matter?" George asked.

Then a third head popped up right behind them. Even before the person pulled off his mask and mouthpiece, I knew who it was.

"Chick!" Delia said, gasping.

"That's right, darlin'," he told her. With one hand, he kept a tight grip on Diego's wet suit. Then he held up the other hand, and I saw the shiny silver blade of a knife.

"Anyone gives me trouble," he said, "and your friend Diego will pay for it."

14

Pirate's Payback

Do whatever he says," Lucy said gravely.

Bess, George, Delia, and I all stood frozen on the deck. Just looking at that gleaming knife blade so close to Diego's throat made my breath catch in my throat.

"How did he get here without us seeing him?" Bess asked.

Even as she said the words, my eyes searched the nearby water. I spotted the fishing boat we'd passed before—a big sporty model with an observation deck and fishing poles angled out in half a dozen spots. What I hadn't noticed before was the small, sun-bleached motorboat that was anchored in the shadow of the larger one.

"His boat's over there," I said, groaning. "He must

have swum underwater the rest of the way."

I guess I spoke a little louder than I had intended, because Chick angled a quick glance up at me. "Nice deduction," he said, keeping his grip on Diego while he kicked his feet to stay afloat. "Of course, it's a little late for guesswork now. Get up on deck, Lucy."

Chick gestured toward the ladder, and Lucy swam over to it and climbed on board. She kept glancing worriedly at Diego as she unstrapped her oxygen tank. Still down in the water, Diego let himself be pulled toward the ladder by Chick.

"Now, lock your friends inside the cabin," Chick instructed, calling up to Lucy. "I don't want any surprise superhero moves from them."

As he spoke, he looked right at me. Okay, I'll admit I was trying to figure out our options. But I wasn't about to do anything stupid—not when Diego's life was at stake. So when Lucy ushered George, Delia, Bess, and me into the cabin, we went.

I noticed that Chick waited until both doors were bolted from the outside before he pushed Diego up the ladder ahead of him. He directed Diego and Lucy over to the rope and pulley and told them to pull up the basket.

"You don't have any right," I heard Diego say as he strained, pulling on the rope. "We've been searching for the *Catarina* for two years! Now that we've found her, you can't just take her treasure from us. It's piracy!"

"Oh, yeah? My folks were treasure hunting these waters two *hundred* years ago," Chick shot back. "I'd say that gives me the right to take anything I want."

"Nothing justifies stealing," I called through the door, before I could stop myself. I knew I should have kept my mouth shut, but Chick's smug, arrogant tone really got to me. "The coral reef could die out, thanks to people like you! Butterfly orchids and other rare plants could become extinct."

Lucy shot me a warning glance. I could tell she was worried about what Chick would do if he got mad. Luckily for us, Chick looked more amused than angry. He just rolled his eyes and said, "Thank you for that touching display of eco-consciousness. Now, hurry up," he added, tapping Diego's shoulder. "The sooner you get the gold up, the sooner I can finish up here."

I saw the scared glances that ricocheted among Bess, George, and Delia. "W-what do you mean, 'finish up'? What are you going to do with us?" Delia asked.

"You'll see," Chick said vaguely.

Call me cynical, but something told me his plans didn't include contacting the coast guard to turn himself in, or letting us go after we promised not to call the police. Our lives were in danger. I had to do something, and buying some time seemed like a good start.

"I have to hand it to you, Chick," I said. "It was pretty clever, the way you gave that phony map to Steve in exchange for all the favors he did for you. He's the one who put the bug on the *Scout*, isn't he?"

Chick glanced toward the cabin before turning back to Lucy and Diego. "Well, it can't hurt to tell you now, since you've figured it out," he said. "Sure, Steve did it."

Delia frowned darkly. Being reminded of what Steve did for Chick in exchange for the map had to hurt. But I needed to keep Chick talking. Out of the corner of my eye, I saw George feel around the computer and sonar. Everything had happened so fast that we hadn't had a chance to search for the listening device. But after a moment, George pulled a small black disk from underneath the table and held it up.

"We know you borrowed Steve Manning's boat when you poached those orchids," Bess added. "Was it a coincidence that you were wearing the same color shirt as him, or did you plan that?"

Chick chuckled to himself. "I figured I might as well look as much like Steve as possible," he told us.

"After all, no one expects me to have a sleek red boat like that one he's got."

"Why not?" I asked. "Didn't you make good money selling all those poached corals and butterfly orchids and things?"

Diego was just hoisting up the wire basket tied to the end of the rope. Half a dozen gold bars were in it. Chick watched greedily while Diego and Lucy lifted the bars out, one by one, and placed them with the others on the deck.

"I got by okay," he said, his eyes still on the gleaming gold. "But I deserve better than that. My family's been elbowed out by all kinds of tourists, coming in with their fancy equipment. If anyone deserves the treasure that's down there," he added, nodding toward the water, "it's me."

"That's why you snuck onto the *Scout* last night, isn't it? Since you had the boat bugged, you knew about the gold bars and coins we found yesterday," George said.

"You got *that* right. I figured, why shouldn't that gold be mine?" Chick said. "I must have missed hearing that your pals the Salazars took the gold with them. That probably happened when my neighbors stopped by to chat."

I could just imagine the kinds of nosy questions the couple from the boat next to Chick's would ask if they heard the conversations that Chick's bug picked up from the *Scout*. Chick definitely would have had to turn it off while they were there.

"Anyhow, after you folks surprised me, I figured I'd be better off waiting for the big payoff, after Lucy and Diego found the mother lode from the *Catarina*," he went on.

"Talk about twisted . . . ," George mumbled under her breath.

I wasn't sure whether Diego and Lucy could tell, but Chick was barely paying any attention to them anymore. As he spoke, he stared at the gold bars in a kind of dreamy trance. I tried to catch Lucy's eye, but she was under the same spell.

Come on! I thought. This is our chance!

Too bad the moment didn't last long. Chick seemed to snap out of his reverie. Turning to look at us with deadly serious eyes, he said, "And now I'm going to get what's coming to me. As soon as this gold is unloaded, I'm afraid you're all going to have a tragic accident."

Chick turned his head for a fraction of a second to glance at the boat Delia and Bess and I had come on. But that was all it took.

Smack!

Diego swung the metal pulley so that it hit Chick on the side of the head. In the next instant,

Chick slumped to the deck, unconscious.

"*That's* what you've got coming to you," Lucy said. She bent over Chick to feel his pulse. "He's still breathing. Quick, get some rope, Diego, so we can tie him up before he comes to."

By the next morning, media hounds from all over the country had arrived in Key Largo. A mob of reporters, cameramen, and staff assistants jammed onto the dock where the *Island Scout* was moored. A couple of them even knocked on Delia's door, trying to get the scoop on the *Catarina's* long-lost treasure and Chick's plot to steal it from the Salazars. By midday it was so crazy that the Salazars decided to hold a press conference.

"Now I know how movie stars feel," Bess joked as she, Delia, George, and I squeezed through the crowd on our way to the *Scout*.

A sea of cameras and reporters and lights closed in around us. Luckily, Lucy and Diego had sent a couple of security guards to accompany us. I don't think we would have made it to the *Scout* without them.

"Over here!" Diego called, waving to us from the front deck as we climbed on board.

He and Lucy were standing next to the treasure from the *Catarina* —a mountain of gold bars, coins, chains, gems, silver candlesticks, plates, cutlery, and belt buckles. Even though I'd seen it the day before, being right next to it still took my breath away.

"Isn't it amazing?" Lucy said. "Diego and I are still pinching ourselves."

"So are we," Bess said, stopping next to the gold. "Now I get why you were so hooked on treasure hunting, George."

Cameras started clicking like crazy, and questions flew from all directions. How much was the treasure worth? Were the Salazars going to put any of it on display for the public? Were they going to search for any more Spanish galleons? Was it true that a modern-day pirate had tried to steal the treasure from them?

"I don't want to romanticize what Chick Russell did," Lucy told reporters. "He broke the law, and he would have hurt us in order to steal the *Catarina*'s treasure. We were just lucky to have friends on board who helped to stop Chick and make sure he wound up in jail, where he belonged."

"And as a token of our thanks, we'd like to present these coins to our friends," Diego went on.

I couldn't believe it when he held up four gold doubloons and handed them to Delia, Bess, George, and me.

The cameras started clicking all over again, and a reporter called out, "What are you going to do with the coins?"

That was an easy one. Bess, George, Delia, and I

put our heads together for just a moment before we answered.

"I'm sure the John Pennekamp Coral Reef State Park could use the money to preserve and protect the reef," I said. "And to protect rare and endangered plants and animals on Key Largo."

That got Delia smiling. And so did the Salazars' announcement that they were donating twenty-five percent of the treasure to the coral reef state park too.

"The money will go a long way toward stopping poachers in the state park," she said, as reporters shouted more questions at Diego and Lucy.

"I hope so," George said. Leaning close to Bess, she added, "Sorry I didn't do more to help track down Chick. I guess I was so awed by the thought of finding the *Catarina* that I didn't understand how bad the poaching problem was. That is, until I saw for myself how far Chick was willing to go to get what he wanted."

"Greed makes people do awful things," Delia said. "Even Steve."

She looked a little sad, and I understood why. Bess and George and I had all been with her when Steve had called the night before to apologize. He'd gone to the police and admitted to putting the bug in the *Scout* for Chick. Since he was cooperating with them, the police were letting him off with community service. Still, Delia had decided she didn't want to date anyone who would help a dangerous con man like Chick.

"I guess Steve's biggest punishment is knowing that if he'd stuck with the Salazars, instead of making that dumb deal with Chick, he'd be getting a cut of the treasure too," Bess said.

"Some people just don't understand," said Delia, "that the biggest treasure is having friends who're there for you when you need them."

It was so true. As I stood there with Bess, George, Delia, and the Salazars, I knew I was the richest person on the planet.

REDISCOVER THE CLASSIC MYSTERIES OF NANCY DREW